PURRFECT MATES, VOLUME 1

Here Kitty, Kitty
My Little Kitty

Joyee Flynn

MENAGE AMOUR

Siren Publishing, Inc.
www.SirenPublishing.com

A SIREN PUBLISHING BOOK
IMPRINT: Ménage Amour

PURRFECT MATES, VOLUME 1
Here Kitty, Kitty
My Little Kitty
Copyright © 2011 by Joyee Flynn

ISBN-10: 1-61034-288-7
ISBN-13: 978-1-61034-288-9

First Printing: March 2011

Cover design by Jinger Heaston
All cover art and logo copyright © 2011 by Siren Publishing, Inc.

Printed in the U.S.A.

PUBLISHER
Siren Publishing, Inc.
www.SirenPublishing.com

DEDICATIONS

Here Kitty, Kitty

To my girl, Brandi: Thanks for coming up with the series name & always being around trying to make me laugh. You're wicked funny, & I appreciate your desire to rule the Evil Minions.

My Little Kitty

To AJ: Thanks for being a great adoptive big bro and always checking up on me. Your morning emails and FB posts crack me up and remind me why we are writers. You truly are my Obe Won and I hope you never change.

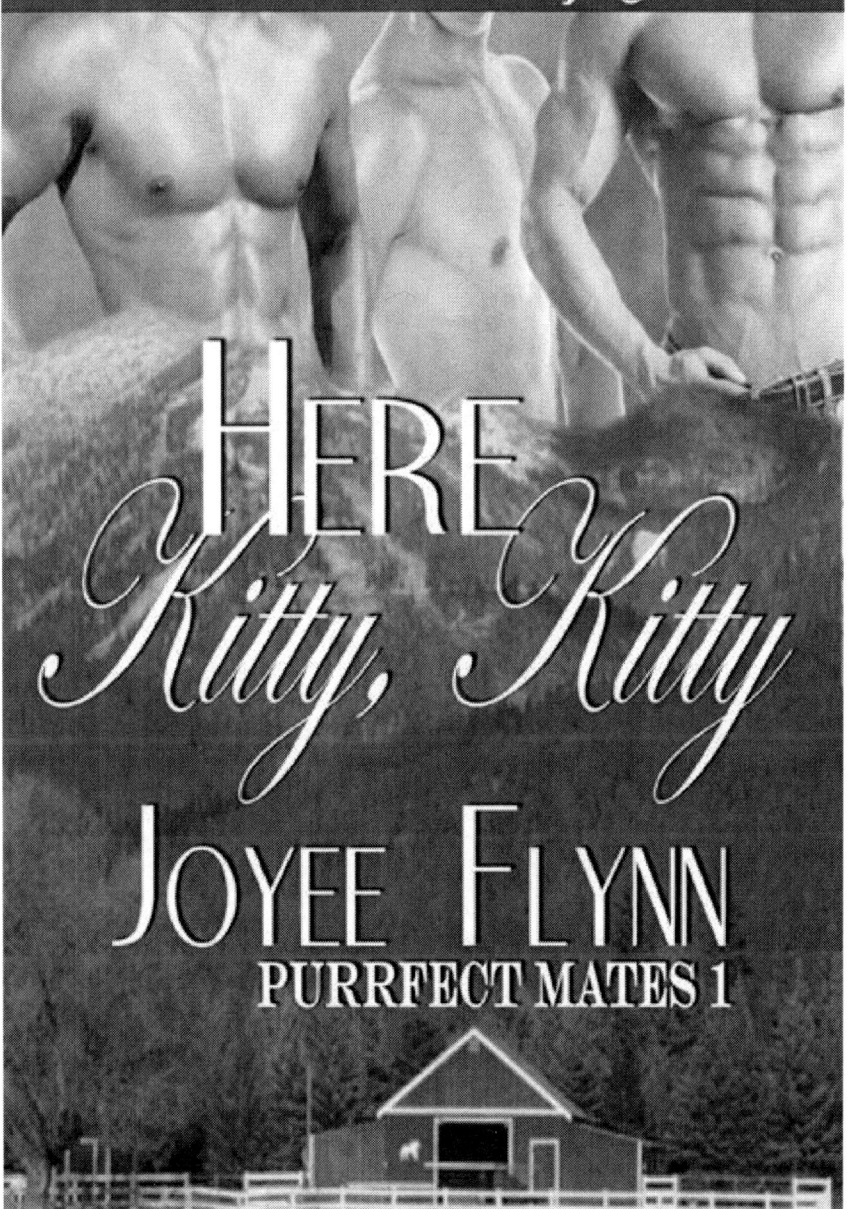

Siren Publishing

Ménage Amour

Here Kitty, Kitty

Joyee Flynn

PURRFECT MATES 1

HERE KITTY, KITTY

Purrfect Mates 1

JOYEE FLYNN
Copyright © 2011

Chapter 1

I had been running for weeks, completely exhausted. This last encounter left me with a bullet in my right shoulder. It had been lodged in my shoulder for days, and the amount of blood loss was starting to worry me. I was running through a small ranch in southern Montana when the smell of my mates hit my nose. Skidding to a stop, I decided to take the biggest risk of my life.

Still in saber form, I limped to the main house that had the lights still on. When I got there, I scratched on the porch loudly. Within moments, two very hot, very large men appeared at the screen door.

"What the fuck?" One gasped as he stared at me. "Tell me I'm hallucinating."

"I don't think you are," the other said as he opened the door. "Because I'm seeing it, too."

"Should I get the gun?" the first one asked, and I went down low on all fours and whimpered. Crawling into the stream of light from the door, I let them see my injury. "Shit, he's hurt. Get the first-aid kit."

"You're going to treat a wounded saber-toothed tiger? Have you lost your fucking mind?" The other one hissed, smacking the first upside the head. I decided it was time and shifted back to human form. When I was done, I collapsed on the ground. "Holy mother in heaven."

"I'm a shifter," I rasped out. It had been so long since I'd used my voice that it felt like my throat had been treated with sandpaper. "There are men after me. I've had the bullet in my shoulder for days, so if you're going to kill me, get it over with. Otherwise, I'm going to bleed out soon."

"You're not going to die," the first said as he came to me, knelt down, and lifted me into his arms. "Ty, get the first-aid kit, towels, hot water. Everything."

"Yeah, I know the drill," Ty answered as he held the door open for us. The first man rushed with me up the stairs and into a bedroom.

"What's your name, little one?" the man asked as he gently laid me on the bed. "I'm Cord Hartwell, and that was Tyson Fitzgerald."

"Avery Donovan, but you can't tell anyone I'm here," I answered. I moaned loudly, feeling myself get hard when he brushed back my hair off my forehead. Any touch from my mates before we've claimed them felt so good it was almost painful.

"We won't tell. You're safe here, Avery," he said gently. I eyed him over, loving what I was seeing now in the well-lit bedroom. He had to be about six four, two eighty-five with shorter blond hair that fell above his eyes, and piercing green eyes.

"You're hot," I coughed out as I started having trouble breathing.

"Hurry up, Ty! I think his lung is collapsing," Cord yelled out. He sat on the bed next to me and kept touching my face. "Hang on, Avery. We can help. We've seen much worse in the military."

"Oh, you're killing me." I groaned, feeling my cock start to leak. "I'm not supposed to be horny right now."

"You are?" Cord asked, his eyes wide as he looked from my face to my groin. "You are. From me?"

"You're kidding, right? You're like my best wet dream," I said through clenched teeth. The pain from my shoulder was starting to radiate outward now that I was in human form. We were able to sustain a lot more damage in saber form, but with the bullet still in me, I wasn't able to heal.

"I'm not gay, Avery," Cord replied, but his eyes told me a very different story.

"My loss," I answered, squinting at him to let him know I wasn't buying it.

"All right, I got what we need," Ty said as he barreled into the room. They moved so they were on either side of me, handing items back and forth and setting up. When it looked like they were ready, Ty leaned over me. "This is going to hurt. We don't have any pain killers."

"Whiskey?" I snickered. "That should help."

"I think we can swing that." Cord chuckled as he got off the bed and left the room. I didn't miss the way Ty's gaze followed him before returning to mine.

"You're as hot as he is," I said, trying to ignore the pain. Ty was about an inch shorter than Cord, but with broader shoulders it seemed. He had to be about the same weight with just as chiseled of a body. Though Ty had dark, dark brown eyes with light brown hair that fell just past his ears.

"Um, thanks," he mumbled as his eyebrows drew together. Ty turned as Cord came back in with the whiskey.

"Bottoms up." Cord snickered as he held the open bottle to my lips. I drank down a few gulps, more out of thirst than desire to drink.

"So, Ty, are you claiming to be straight, too?" I asked as he started working on the hole in my shoulder.

"I am straight," Ty replied, not even glancing up at me. "How long did you say you had this bullet in your shoulder? It looks like weeks."

"A few days. I kept reopening it with my claws otherwise the skin would have healed over it, and I'd be fucked." I hissed out. "You guys better realize you're not straight in the next couple of days, or I'm majorly screwed."

"What does us being gay or straight have to do with you?" Cord asked as he handed Ty some gauze. Just then, Ty sliced the wound open wider, and I screamed out in pain. They both held me down as the pain passed a bit.

"If I don't claim you in about three days or so, I'll die," I panted out, trying to focus on anything but the pain.

"What?" they both asked, staring at me. Unfortunately, Ty still had the knife in my wound, and he jerked it to the side.

"Fuck, that hurts," I cried out as black dots started to swarm my vision.

"Shit, sorry." Ty cursed as he focused back on what he was doing. When he started digging out the bullet, everything went fuzzy, then black.

* * * *

"What did he mean that he'd die?" I heard Ty ask as I awoke.

"Dude, he was in pain and losing major amounts of blood," Cord answered as I opened my eyes. They were standing at the edge of the bed, cleaning up the mess from my makeshift surgery.

"Doesn't mean what I said wasn't true," I croaked out, watching as they both jumped in surprise and turned toward me.

"How are you awake already?" Ty asked, eyes wide.

"I heal faster than you do," I answered, trying to sit up.

"Even so, lay still," Cord said, coming toward me and resting his hand on my good shoulder.

"I need to shift so I can mend quicker," I replied, eyeing him over. "Do you want me to do to it outside?"

"You really are a shape-shifter, aren't you?" he asked quietly. "But there's no such thing."

"I beg to differ." I snickered as I pushed myself up. "Is it okay if I do it in here?"

"That depends," Ty answered slowly. "Do you know that you are you when you shift? I mean, are you just an animal?"

"No, I'm completely sentient when I change," I replied. "I knew you were my mates when I approached the house."

"Your mates?" They both gasped at the same time.

"Yes, my mates." I giggled. "I'll explain everything after I shift and get the healing process going, okay?"

They shared a skeptical look before turning back to me and nodding. I threw off the sheet, got out of bed, and got on all fours. Then I let the change over take me, and seconds later I was in saber form.

"Fuck me," Ty whispered.

I'd like to, I thought to myself, smiling. Cord stood up and slowly approached me. Ty did the same until they were right in front of me on their knees. Not sure what to do, I tilted my head and licked Cord's face.

"Shit, your tongue is rough." He chuckled as he scratched behind my ear. "It's strange enough that you're a shape-shifter, but you change into an extinct animal to top it off."

"You're absolutely breathtaking though," Ty whispered as he reached out and touched my neck. Running his hands down my flank, he kept his movements very slow. It felt like heaven, and I let out a loud purr.

"I think he likes that." Cord snickered. I nodded my head and flopped over to my back, exposing my belly to them. "Are we supposed to rub his stomach like a dog?"

"Do I look like I know?" Ty asked, glancing at Cord like he'd fallen off his rocker. I lifted my head and licked Ty's face, as well. He busted out laughing and scratched my stomach. "His fur is so soft."

"I can't believe this is happening," Cord whispered, his eyes never leaving me. I figured this was about as good of time as any and shifted back. Their eyes went wide as they watched, frozen in shock.

"You don't have to stop rubbing my tummy." I purred playfully. "It felt fantastic."

"It's weird now that you're a man again," Ty replied gently, but I saw his erection in his shorts. Slowly getting up, I moved to straddle his lap and licked along his neck.

"I think you like the idea of touching me when I'm like this," I whispered in his ear.

"Stop, I told you I was straight," Ty said, not sounding happy with me. I backed off and saw he was shaking, partly from anger, but I saw the lust in his eyes, as well.

"Your shoulder's healed," Cord said, clearing his throat. I glanced down and saw he was right. Gazing back at him, I noticed he seemed to like what I'd done to Ty, as well. "So you're a saber-toothed tiger shifter."

"Yup." I nodded, not knowing what else to do.

"You said we were your mates?" Ty asked, raising an eyebrow at me.

"I was running through your ranch, and I smelled my mates." I shrugged, glad it didn't hurt to do that anymore. "I took a chance that you would help me and not just shoot me. I mean, if I can't trust my mates, who can I trust?"

"We're not your mates," Cord said gently, glancing at Ty. "Ty and I have been friends since high school. We took over the ranch a few years ago when his parents died. My parents died when I was young, and Ty's parents took me in."

"I'm sorry," I replied as I took each of their hands in mine. "I know losing family is hard."

"Where is your family?" Ty asked, staring at our joined hands.

"I don't know. I've not seen them in years."

"Why not?" Cord asked, seeming to be in the same trance as his gaze never left our hands.

"I'll answer whatever questions you guys want, but I have one request first."

"What would that be?" Ty smiled, raising an eyebrow at me.

"Feed me. I'm starving and so thirsty it's not even funny," I begged.

"Oh, shit, sorry. We should have thought of that," Cord replied and immediately stood up, dropping my hand.

"I think you were a little busy with the very large, extinct tiger that showed up on your door step." I giggled as Ty stood and helped me up. When he went to let go of my hand, I squeezed it tighter. He looked uncomfortable, eyes darting to and from me, but he didn't let go. They led me downstairs and into the kitchen.

"What do you like to eat?" Cord asked as he opened the fridge.

"Cock," I answered sweetly. Ty let go of my hand and coughed like he was choking as Cord just stood there with his mouth hanging open. "What? You asked."

"What do you like for food?" Cord replied, tilting his head and smirking at me.

"Anything with meat." I snickered, loving that Cord was playful as Ty was trying to regain his composure. "No, seriously, I'm not picky."

"Okay, I'll find something while you explain to us this mating thing," he said. I watched his large, muscled body move for a moment before I snapped out of it and sat down. Ty sat in the chair next to me, blushing when I caught him checking my lithe body out. His gazed shifted down to my hard dick again before returning to my face.

"I want to try something first," I replied quietly as I stood up and moved toward Ty. He stared into my eyes as I spread my legs and stood on either side of his. I slowly sat down, trying to not break the trance he seemed to be in. Leaning forward, I pressed my lips to his. At first, he stayed stiff and didn't respond, but when I scooted forward and my dick pushed into his stomach, it was like he snapped. Grabbing my ass, he pulled me closer and licked my lips.

Moaning, I wrapped my arms around his neck and melted into the kiss. When he gasped, I took full advantage and slid my tongue into his mouth. I felt him get hard under my ass and started to rub my hips over his growing erection.

"Wait, I'm not gay," he panted as he pulled away.

"I think you're at least bisexual," I whispered against his lips before diving into another kiss. He squeezed my ass as he moved me so our groins rubbed against each other.

"Fuck." Cord hissed. We broke apart and turned toward him. Cord's erection looked like it was going to break out of his jeans.

"Enjoying this?" I asked, nodding toward his hard-on.

"I've just never seen…" he stuttered, trailing off. I got up off Ty's lap and boldly walked over to Cord. Placing my hands on his chest, I ran my hands down his body until I got to his groin.

"Maybe not, but you liked it." I purred as I squeezed his cock through his pants. I wasn't normally this forward with the men I was attracted to, but these were my mates, and I had less than forty-eight hours to claim them before I went into heat. Cord groaned as I kept massaging his crotch. "Can I keep going?"

"And do what?" he panted, staring down at me. I wasn't more than five seven, so both of them towered over me.

"Anything you'd let me do without making you feel uncomfortable," I said gently. He glanced over at Ty before looking back at me. "Ty can join us."

"I've never wanted a man before," Cord whispered, turning bright red. We both knew he was lying through his teeth, but I wasn't about to call him out on it.

"I'm your mate. You can't help yourself even if you wanted to," I explained. "Fate picked both of you out for me. I knew it the moment I smelled you. There's nothing wrong with being with a man."

"I know that," he mumbled, his eyes glazing over as I squeezed him harder. "I'm just not sure what to do."

"Do you want me?" I asked. He pursed his lips together in thought a moment before silently nodding. "Then do whatever you want to me. I want you, too."

Seconds after I finished, he mashed his mouth on mine. I gasped in surprise, not thinking he would be so forward. His sweet lips were softer than they looked. I melted into him and let out a small yelp as he lifted me up. Instinctively, I wrapped my arms and legs around him as his hands moved under my ass.

"Ty wants you as much as you want him, Cord," I whispered in his ear as we broke apart. "The only people you're kidding are each other. I see the way you look at him."

"Do you really think so?" he asked quietly.

"Yeah, I do," I answered, glancing over my shoulder at Ty. The heated look he was giving us was enough to set the kitchen on fire. I reached my hand out to him. "Join us."

"I'm fine here," Ty mumbled.

"Please, Ty," Cord said softly. Ty's head shot in his direction, shock all over his face.

"You want me, Cord?" he asked, his jaw just about on the floor.

"For so long," Cord answered, moaning when I started to rub my groin against his.

"Why didn't you ever say anything?" Ty replied as he cautiously stood and moved toward us.

"Why didn't you?" Cord answered defensively. I had an inkling this was going to go south really fast. "All these years, I thought I was nuts for loving you. Then Avery shows up, and both of us suddenly aren't acting very straight."

"I didn't mean to start a fight," I said softly as I lowered myself to my feet. "I'm working on a deadline here. I don't have time to beat around the bush."

"What do you mean 'deadline?'" Ty growled, turning his anger at me.

"I have forty-eight hours from when I smelled my mates to claim them," I answered, not liking the looks they were giving me. "After that, I go into heat, and if I've claimed them, it's fun and sex-a-palooza. If not, I start to overheat and die within a couple of days."

"So, if one of us doesn't want to be with you and won't let you claim us, you die," Cord stated, obviously not believing me. "Sounds like a horrible pickup line to trap people into a relationship."

"And why do you get two mates?" Ty threw in, seeming just as disbelieving and pissed off. "I mean, why did we get so lucky that you come in here, say you only have a couple of days, and throw our lives into upheaval?"

"I—I didn't mean," I started to stammer, but they were standing shoulder to shoulder, completely pissed off and focusing on me. As I started to shake, I knew I was about to shift. It was instinct that I do so whenever I felt threatened or unsafe.

"You meant to," Cord scoffed as he stepped toward me. "You came in here flaunting your hot little body, knowing full well that we said we were straight."

"But you're not," I whispered as I felt tears burning in my eyes.

"That's not for *you* to decide," Ty replied, crossing his arms over his chest. "We were happy with the way things were. But you didn't care about that, did you, Avery? No, it's all about you and what you need. Not that we even believe you."

"You show up here, a shape-shifter, for god sakes," Cord continued. "With a bullet in your shoulder. We don't even know how that happened. Demanding we're your mates and are gay and after thirty-something years of being straight, you expect to snap your fingers and get your way."

"It wasn't like that," I sniffled as I took a step back.

"That's *exactly* how it was," Ty yelled. "So, because of some freak twist of fate, we're stuck being mated to a goddamn shape-shifter?"

"I'm sorry," I cried out as the change over took me. They both gasped as I shifted, turned, and ran. I got to the front door and realized they had closed it. There wasn't just the screen door anymore.

"Avery, get back here," Cord yelled out angrily. On instinct, I turned around to face him and snarled loudly.

"Cord, back off. He feels cornered," Ty said, grabbing Cord's arm. He slowly moved toward the door as I backed away to let him. I never took my eyes off Cord, as well, whose hands were in fists at his side. Ty unlocked and opened the main door, before holding open the screen door. As soon as I saw the out, I took it. I ran past him, careful not to knock him over. Once out the door and on the porch, I sprinted away from the house.

What now? I asked myself. I knew they were pissed, but if I ran away, I would die in a few days. If I kept going on the run by myself, the hunters would get me. Of all the reactions I'd ever expected when I finally found my mates, *that* wasn't one of them. I got that it was shocking and a lot to take in, but, wow, did they think I was full of shit.

After a few minutes' run, I was over a mile from the house. Slowing down, I found a soft-looking patch of grass hidden by some bushes. I lay down, trying to figure out what to do now. My heart was breaking as I realized that my mates didn't want me. To top it off, I was still exhausted, hungry, and thirsty, and my shoulder hurt. I couldn't shift back when my emotions were all over the place like this. Instead, I closed my eyes and decided to at least get some rest.

At first, I couldn't since I was completely overcome with grief. I'd never cried in saber form before, but the tears kept coming. It didn't even seem to matter as much that I was going to die as the fact that they didn't want me. That was the last thought I had as I finally drifted off.

Chapter 2

"Shit, Ty, he's freezing cold," Cord said as I felt myself being lifted up. My eyes flew open as I squirmed out of his grasp. Landing on my feet, I took several steps back.

"I said I was sorry," I mumbled as my teeth chattered. The temperature had to have dropped at least twenty degrees since I'd come back outside. I was guessing it was under fifty now, and I was naked.

"We're sorry, Avery," Cord answered as he approached me slowly. "Ty and I talked, and we're not mad at you. Confused and not sure what to do, but none of this is your fault."

"It's not?" I asked, glancing between him and Ty. "If I hadn't shown up—"

"Cord and I would still be lying to each other about how we feel," Ty finished. "We won't yell or hurt you, Avery. Let's all just go inside, okay? You need to eat, and you've been injured. Whether you heal fast or not, you need rest."

"I'm sorry I shifted. It's instinct for me when I feel threatened or scared," I whispered.

"We figured that out later," Cord said as he reached for me. I flinched, but then felt dizzy enough to grab onto him. As I swayed on my feet, Cord quickly swept me up into his arms. "Let's get back home and feed you."

"Okay," I answered, still freezing but snuggling up against him. Ty took off his jacket before climbing into the truck. Cord passed me to him, and Ty snuggled me close as he pulled the coat around me. I buried my face in his neck and inhaled deeply. "God, you smell good."

"Thanks, I think." Ty chuckled as he leaned over and rested his forehead against mine. "You're going to have to be patient with us, Avery. We've never been with a man before, and I've not even been attracted to anyone but Cord."

"Oh, fuck, you're killing me." I moaned as I wrapped my arms around his neck. I pulled his head down and kissed him gently.

"How so?" Ty whispered against my lips.

"Knowing that no other man has been with you," I answered, surprised that he didn't get it. "That Cord and I are going to be the only men who have ever had you."

"That's hot?" he asked, brows drawing together.

"I think so." Cord chuckled as he started up the truck and threw it in drive. "Can we ask how you got shot, Avery?"

"Hunters," I answered quietly. Thinking about it for a moment, I decided we weren't going to get anywhere if I wasn't completely honest with them. "There are humans out there that know about my kind. Some want us dead because they think we're unnatural. Others want us for trophies."

"Trophies?" Ty asked.

"If we die in saber form, we stay that way," I whispered, another shiver going through me. "They are extreme hunters that want to stuff us or mount us for their collection."

"Do they know that you're human?" he asked gently. I searched his face and realized he was serious. He thought of me as human.

"Thank you," I said as I sat up on his lap and hugged him fiercely.

"For what?" Ty chuckled.

"For calling me human," I answered, feeling my cheeks heat up. "I thought you might always see me as a freak."

"You're not a freak, Avery," Cord said firmly as we pulled up to the house. "Different, yes. Freak, no way. We were talking about a strange twist of fate when we said that—not that you were a freak."

"They know I'm a man," I replied, answering Ty's earlier question. "I'm either not human to them, or they don't care."

"We won't let them hurt you, baby," Ty stated as he climbed out of the truck. I wrapped my arms and legs around him as he walked toward the house. As he moved, his shorts-covered cock rubbed against my ass. I groaned loudly, moving my hips so that my dick pushed against his stomach. "Do you ever stop?"

"I can't. You're my mate." I hissed as I continued to hump his hips. "It feels so good it almost hurts. I can't get enough."

"Is this like marking us with your scent?" Cord asked. He opened the door for us, and I caught the look of lust he gave us.

"Partially. Please touch me, Cord," I begged, reaching for his hand. He moved so that he sandwiched me against Ty. I leaned back, laying my head on his shoulder as I kept moving my hips over Ty's. "I'm sorry, I can't control it. It's like I have this itch that only you guys can scratch."

"What can we do, Avery?" Ty gasped out, his hands moving to my ass.

"Touch me, please. Anywhere. everywhere," I whimpered and begged.

"You are so fucking beautiful." Cord hissed out as he licked my neck. "Let's move this to the couch."

"Please, yes. I need you both so badly," I cried out, feeling as if I was going to burst into flames. Ty quickly brought us into the living room and sat down on the couch with me on his lap. Before I'd even realized it, my hands had shifted into claws and I was slicing off his clothes. He gasped in surprise, but I'd been careful not to cut him. Once he was naked, I mashed my lips down on his, squirming all over his body. I couldn't touch enough of him fast enough.

"You guys are making me hard," Cord said as he sat down next to us. I moved in a flash onto him and shredded his clothes, as well. "Wow, you really are a horny little one, aren't you, baby?"

"I can't control it." I moaned as I slid down his body between his knees. His huge, ten-inch cock was standing up straight in front of my face. Without even thinking about it, I swallowed down as much of it as I could.

"Fuck," Cord gasped out, touching my head gently as I sucked him off.

"More. I need more. Please, touch me, Ty," I begged before wrapping my lips around Cord's cock again.

"Where?" Ty asked, sounding shocked.

"I don't know." Cord moaned. "Get behind him. His skin's heating up."

Ty scrambled off the couch and surrounded my smaller body with his. Cord spread his legs wider to accommodate both of us. Ty reached down and stroked my dick as his other hand wrapped around my chest. I moaned loudly, thrusting into his hand as I swallowed Cord's cock over and over again.

"Fuck, I'm going to come, baby." Cord hissed out. He stiffened up and cried out as he shot his seed down my throat. I swallowed mouthful after mouthful of it greedily, loving the taste of my mate. As soon as he was spent, I spun around and pushed Ty onto his back. I lay over him, making sure our cocks were rubbing together and dry fucked him like I had never done with another before.

"Don't stop, baby." Ty moaned, his eyes just about rolling back into his head. I growled loudly, loving that I was making my mate so happy. Leaning over, I took one of his nipples between my lips and bit down. "Oh, shit! Fuck, Avery, just like that."

"You guys are going to make me hard again," Cord panted, still trying to catch his breath. I ground my hips hard against Ty's, loving the feel of his body. We both cried out as we climaxed together, the space between us filling up with our combined cum.

"Thank you, thank you," I chanted over and over again as I came and even after I was spent. It felt like I'd been dumped in a cold bath after spending too much time in the sun and was extremely burnt. I lay there on top of Ty like a wet noodle, my exhaustion taking over my need to feel my mates.

"Are you okay, Avery?" Cord asked as he knelt down by me. I couldn't even lift my head. Gazing up at him, I smiled.

"Tired, hungry, and thirsty," I panted out. "But I finally don't feel like I'm going to claw off my skin with need for you guys."

"Well, that's a step in the right direction, I guess." Ty chuckled under me.

"I think feeding you is in order after getting the best blowjob ever." Cord winked at me. He lifted me up into his arms effortlessly and brought us into the kitchen. Gently setting me on the counter, he kissed me gently. I leaned back against the cabinet still feeling as if I was going to collapse. He looked me over for a moment before racing over to the fridge.

"Shit, you don't look good, baby," Ty said as he walked over toward me. He grabbed the sports drink from Cord and helped me drink it down. It tasted like sugary bliss. He made me go slowly, only a few sips at a time.

"I've been on the run for weeks," I answered as I finished the drink. "I've only eaten a couple of rabbits along the way."

"Rabbits?" Cord asked, raising an eyebrow at me.

"I was in saber form." I shrugged. "This is the longest I've been in human form for years."

"My god, why?" Ty replied as his eyes went wide.

"Can we not talk about that yet?" I asked, feeling the tears burn at my eyes.

"It's okay. We can shelf it for now," Ty said gently as he wiped away the first tears. He lifted me up in his arms, went over to the table, and sat down with me in his lap. Running his hands over my arms, he tried to calm me down. "You're safe now, Avery. We won't let anyone hurt you."

"I brought trouble right to you," I whispered as the tears started falling freely. "They won't stop, ever."

"Then good thing fate gave you two ex-Marines." Cord chuckled as he scrambled up some eggs. "We can take care of this, baby."

"I'm so sorry," I hiccupped.

"Hey, now, we were enjoying our post-orgasm glow," Ty soothed. "Let's not get into the heavy stuff until tomorrow. It's late. You need to eat and get some rest, okay, baby?"

I sniffled and tried to get my emotions under control as I gazed up at him. "Fate gave me the best mates ever," I said, wrapping my arms around his neck.

"We need to talk about that, Avery," Cord replied gently as he put plates of food on the table. My stomach growled loudly as I turned away from Ty and grabbed some toast. Stuffing it in my mouth, I scooped some eggs up with my hands and ate those as well.

"Sorry," I said after I swallowed. Cord was staring at me like I'd grown another head. "It's been so long since I've had anything besides raw meat."

"I'm glad you like it." He chuckled as he handed me a fork. I wiped my hands off on the paper towels he'd given me and took it from him. It felt so foreign in my hands. Every time I tried to scoop up some food, it fell right back off the fork. After trying several times, I screamed in frustration and threw the fork across the kitchen.

"Sorry," I whispered when I calmed down.

"Hey, it's okay," Ty said as he ran his hands over my arms. "We'll figure this out, Avery. You've been through a lot."

"I've got an idea." Cord smirked. He grabbed a couple pieces of toast, scooped some eggs on them, and made me a sandwich. I took it from him gratefully, his kindness warmed my heart.

"Thank you," I said before snarfing it down. "I really do have the best mates."

"So is being mated like being married?" Ty asked as I kept eating.

"In a way, but it's an unbreakable bond unless I die," I answered with a mouthful of food. "But it comes with perks."

"Like?" Cord asked, raising an eyebrow.

"How old do you think I am?" I smirked at him. I knew I looked like a twenty-year-old twink, but that was the furthest from the truth.

"Twenty maybe?" he answered, looking confused.

"I'm going to be forty-six in a month." I giggled, loving his shocked look. "I age slower than humans. I'm stronger, faster, heal quicker, and, if you mate me, you will, too."

"Wow." Ty whistled. Cord wiped his hands over his face. "And what about this going into heat thing?"

"Once a month, I go into heat during the lunar cycle," I explained. Cord handed me another egg sandwich which I immediately bit into. "That's part of why we each have two mates. The moon effects all weres—wolves turn furry, tigers and cats go into heat. I will fuck, suck, bite, lick every inch of my mates for three days."

"Oh, hell," Cord groaned, lust filling his eyes. "And this is every month? Not just after we mate?"

"The heat I go through after mating is stronger." I giggled, feeling myself get hard. "Right now, I want you so bad it's almost like a fire inside me urging me to claim you. After I do, we call it the honeymoon heat. I'll be this insatiable horn dog, and it will affect you, too. Both of you. None of us will get enough of each other."

"Okay, then," Ty said, clearing his throat. I felt him get hard underneath me.

"I think my big mate likes the idea," I purred as I squirmed on his lap.

"Yes, but we need to talk right now." He moaned as he held my hips still. In a flash, I moved to another chair across the table from them. Both of them stared at me with open mouths.

"Sorry. When you touch me like that, I can't think." I snickered. "All I can think about is fucking and claiming you."

"It's going to take some getting used to that you can move that fast," Cord said slowly. He glanced over at Ty who simply nodded his head. "So, you're saying if we let you claim us, we'll be able to move like that, too?"

"Yes," I whispered, lowering my sandwich to the table. I stared at my hands for a few moments before looking up to meet their gazes. "Is that the only reason you'd want to keep me?"

"No," they both said loudly. Ty put his hand over Cord's arm and continued, "We're just trying to figure this out, Avery. This morning, we were normal ranchers. Then we find a saber-toothed tiger shifter, and now there's a whole world we know nothing about. I didn't miss the part where you said there were other weres, like wolves and what not."

"Vampires are real, too, but they can go out in sunlight." I shrugged. I stopped when Cord held up a hand and went back to my sandwich.

"Let's stick with the necessary details for now," Cord said gently. "I'm trying not to freak out and overload. You said that you have forty-eight hours to claim us before you get sick. That doesn't give us much time to make the biggest decision of our lives, Avery."

"I understand," I replied quietly, not looking at either one of them. We were quiet as I finished my sandwich. Then an idea hit me. "Can I take a shower? It's been years since I've not just cleaned off in a pond or someone hosed me off."

"We're going to have to talk about that tomorrow, Avery," Ty said. I nodded, understanding that the curiosity had to be killing them. "I'll show you how to work the shower."

"Thank you for being so patient with me and not tossing me out on my ass," I replied as I got up from the table.

"None of this is your fault, Avery. And I have this need to protect you at all costs," Cord answered as he started to clean up.

"That's because you're my mate," I whispered. "It's ingrained in you to want to take care of and protect me."

"Is that why we're attracted to you, too?" Ty asked.

"No," I answered, closing my eyes and taking a deep breath. When I opened them, they were both staring at me. "You might feel drawn to me, but fate can't make you attracted to me. Between the draw to each other and the need to care for me, you might move more quickly than you normally would. But what you're feeling is real."

"So the overwhelming desire to touch you is how I really feel?" Cord asked as he took a step toward me.

"Yes, just stronger than you'd feel with someone you were just attracted to." I nodded. "The same with Ty. You're not just my mates. You're each other's mates as well. What you feel is more than just friendship."

"Since the moment I met him," Cord whispered, reaching out and touching my cheek. "But you were the missing piece, Avery. You brought us together, made us face how we felt."

"I don't know whether to apologize or say you're welcome," I answered, confused.

"Thank you," Ty said as he leaned over and kissed me. When he lifted his head, Cord's lips replaced his.

"Can you give us some time to talk while you shower?" Cord asked when we parted. I nodded like an idiot. He smiled down at me as he lifted me into his arms and walked us up the stairs and into the bathroom. Setting me on my feet, he showed me how to turn the shower on and adjust the temperature. "I want to say yes, Avery. Everything inside me is screaming to have you claim me and keep you forever."

"But?" I whispered.

"But this is a lot really fast," he answered as he handed the soap. "And it's a lot of pressure knowing you'll die if I say no. I just need to think."

"I understand," I replied, stepping into the shower and running the soap over my body. I knew I was being a shit as I soaped up my groin and stroked my cock as he stared at me. "I've had all my life to prepare for finding my mates. You've had a few hours."

"You are the hottest little thing I've ever fucking seen." Cord hissed. I saw his body responding to mine, and I started to feel guilty.

"I'm sorry, it's mean to tease you," I said as I turned away from him. He growled loudly, and I felt his hands on me.

"Yeah, showing me that firm little ass is much better." He hissed as he licked along my neck. I moaned, melting into him as I tilted my head to give him better access. "You have to fuck us when you claim us, right?"

"Yes," I purred as his hands ran over my stomach and chest. "I'll shift into half cat, half man and bite your neck while I fuck your gorgeous ass."

"You're going to be the death of me." He groaned, and I froze up.

"It won't kill you." I gasped as I spun in his arms and stared at him. "I won't ever let anyone hurt you guys. No one's stupid enough to fuck with a tiger's mates."

"No, I didn't mean that literally," Cord said as he took my face in his hands. "It's an expression."

"Oh, sorry," I replied, feeling my face heating up.

"It's hot when you blush, you little imp." He purred as he leaned over and kissed me. Cord pulled away before I could yank him into the shower with me. "You get clean. Ty and I are going to go talk."

"Can't we all shower together instead?" I pouted. "I might get lonely in here."

"We can all shower another time." He chuckled as he closed the glass door. "We're on a timetable."

"Fine, but I might be a while." I groaned as I stepped back under the water. He laughed as he left the bathroom. The hot water felt fucking fantastic as it ran over my exhausted muscles. I took my sweet time getting clean before moving to shampoo my hair. When the water started to run cold, I turned it off and got out. I shook off the water on me before walking back into the bedroom.

"Want a towel?" Ty asked with a smirk.

"What?" I replied, not understanding what he was getting at. "I shook dry."

They exchanged a look before bursting out laughing. I felt my entire body heat up with embarrassment. But then I got mad. It wasn't right that they were laughing at me when I didn't know any better.

"Fuck you both," I yelled, feeling tears burning my eyes as I ran from the room. I didn't know the house well, and my tears were blurring my vision, so when I got down two stairs, I tripped. Screaming as I fell down the flight of stairs, I landed at the bottom in a heap. They came flying down the stairs after me, trying to help. "Leave me alone! I'm not some freak you can just laugh at."

"Avery, we're sorry. We weren't laughing at you," Cord said as he tried to pull me into his arms.

"I wasn't laughing, so you weren't laughing *with* me." I growled, my ankle throbbing.

"Yeah, but we were laughing at how cute you were," Ty said gently as I tried to drag myself away from them. "It's adorable how you don't know the normal way to do things."

"Because I was caged in captivity for almost thirty years!" I screamed. They both stared at me with wide eyes as I started crying. "I was running in the woods with my family when I was fourteen and some hunters got me. They caged me, and I stayed in saber form for the next twenty-nine years until I was able to escape a month ago."

"Fuck," Cord whispered as his hand went over his mouth.

"I don't know if my family is dead or alive," I cried, tears flowing freely now. "They kept me in some freak show in a circus doing tricks, knowing full well I was a shifter. They whipped me when I wouldn't perform. When I was too tired to stay in saber form, they raped me. So I tried as hard as I could to always stay in that form."

"Jesus, baby," Ty said as he pulled me to him. I was still upset with them, but right then I needed the comfort my mates could only give me. Wrapping my arms around his neck, I cried out when I went to use my ankle. "We're so sorry. We really weren't laughing at you, Avery. You're just so innocent in certain ways. It's so endearing. We laughed because we were shocked that you just shook off the water, standing there hot and naked without getting what we meant about using a towel."

"Please don't laugh at me anymore." I hiccupped, burying my face in his neck. "I can't help what I don't know."

"We won't," Cord whispered as he moved behind me to hug both of us. "We don't think you're a freak or someone to laugh at. You're amazing and gorgeous."

"Really?" I gasped, looking over my shoulder at him.

"Really," he said before he leaned down and claimed my lips. I moaned and melted into them. "We want you, Avery. We talked it over and decided that there's no way we're going to let you out of our lives now that we've found you."

"Really?" I whispered as the tears started up again. "I can stay here with you guys forever? You want me after what I just told you?"

"Even more now," Ty answered. "You're amazing and special and have been through more than either of us can even imagine. This is much faster than we would have liked, but we both feel we would have wanted you with us. And with the timetable, we aren't willing to risk losing you."

"So you're saying yes so that I won't die? That's not why I want you to mate with me," I replied, pulling away from them.

"No, that's not what we're saying," Cord yelled, grabbing my shoulders firmly. "We want you, Avery. All of you. Yes, we're saying yes faster than maybe we would have if we weren't on a deadline, but that isn't why we want you."

I nodded as I moved out of their arms and lay on my side. Shifting into tiger form so I would heal my ankle, I then shifted into half tiger, half man. In tiger form, I was close to four hundred fifty pounds, but in half form I was almost as tall as they were. I weighed close to two fifty and was covered in fur. "You want this?" I asked as I stood up.

"Yes," the both said as they got to their feet. I froze as they surrounded me with their arms and bodies.

"This is where you belong, Avery," Ty said gently. I stared into his eyes before turning to Cord and doing the same. Shifting back to my smaller form, they instantly moved closer to me now that I didn't take up as much room.

"Let's get some sleep, baby." Cord smiled at me. He lifted me up into his arms, and I wrapped myself around him. No one said a word as we made our way upstairs and into Cord's bedroom.

"We're going to need a bigger bed." I giggled as he laid me down in the middle.

"We don't normally share a bed." Ty snickered as they climbed in on either side of me. "But if we keep the full size bed, we'll always have to sleep on top of each other."

"I'd prefer that we can do that without risking rolling off the bed," Cord said as he spooned the back of me. "We'll order a bigger bed tomorrow, baby."

"I don't have any money," I whispered.

"Don't worry, we do." Ty chuckled before kissing my lips. When I went to say something, both of them covered my mouth with their hands and laughed. "Don't even worry about it, okay? We've got enough on our plates."

"Okay, but I want to help out and pull my weight," I said as I kissed both of their hands.

"Deal." Cord chuckled as he nestled his head in my neck. I closed my eyes and felt more at peace then I could ever remember. I'd found my mates, and they were going to keep me.

Chapter 3

I woke up the next morning in between my mates and my skin feeling like it was on fire. Crawling out of bed as fast as I could without waking them, I booked it to the bathroom. I tried to remember how to work the shower, I turned it on full blast cold and got under the spray. It hadn't even been a full twenty-four hours since I'd met them. Why was this getting worse for me?

Once I was freezing, I sat on the floor of the shower and wrapped my arms around my knees. Thinking back to what I'd been told about mating, I couldn't fill in the blanks. It had been so long ago since my parents explained any of it to me and, since I'd been only fourteen, I was pretty sure they didn't tell me everything.

"Avery, are you okay?" Ty asked as he and Cord opened the door to the shower. I looked up, and whatever was on my face must have been enough to tell them I was far from fine. As they stepped into the shower toward me, I scrambled away and pressed against the far back wall.

"It's worse today. I don't know what's going on," I panted holding my hands out in front of me. "I'm trying to remember everything I know about mating, but I learned it all so long ago."

"Then claim us," Cord said gently as he shared a look with Ty. He nodded in agreement as Cord held his arms open to me. "We're ready, Avery. Well, maybe not ready, but it's killing me to see you like this. If claiming us will alleviate this, then we can do it now."

"No, I won't force you," I cried, shaking my head. "I can hold out until you're ready."

"Avery, I'm not sure we'll ever be ready," Ty said gently. He got down on all fours and crawled to me, his boxers getting soaked. "I don't know about Cord, but I'm scared. Last night was the first time I'd even touched a man, and I'm nervous."

"I'm so sorry," I whispered. "You have to stay away from me. I'm holding on by a thread here."

"No, we won't leave you to suffer like this," Ty replied, tears filling his eyes. "I'd rather deal with my fears and work through this together than watch you hurting, sitting in a freezing shower so you don't jump us."

"I'm scared," I said, turning my face into his hand when he cupped my cheek. "I don't know what's happening to me."

"We'll figure it out," he whispered. He leaned in to kiss me, and my control snapped. I jumped him, knocking him on his back as I claimed his lips. Cord must have shut off the water because the freezing spray stopped. I molded my body to Ty's as I stared down in his eyes.

"Mine," I growled before smashing my mouth down on his. He wrapped his arms around me as I started humping his groin.

"Let's get into bed, Avery," Cord said gently. As soon as he touched my shoulder, I leapt up and wrapped my body around his. He staggered out of the shower as I tore off his boxers. I nibbled and licked his neck as he moaned and quickly got us to the bed.

"Lube, now." I hissed when I felt him get hard. He lowered me to the bed, and I rolled us over so he was on the bottom.

"I don't think we have any," he panted, looking up at me with wide eyes.

"Get me something that works. Otherwise, I might hurt you." I snarled as I pinned him down. He went to move, gasping when he realized I was too strong to get away. "Don't panic. It turns me on. I'm trying to keep some shred of control here."

"I've got lube in my room," Ty said from behind us. I slowly released Cord's arms and started kissing down his body. My tiger was dying to be released and claim his mate. I knew I couldn't fight him and my urge to fuck Cord. Letting the half shift over take me, I used my larger tongue to please my mate.

"Oh, fuck, baby," he screamed as I licked his balls. "Your tongue feels amazing."

"You've not seen the half of what I can do." I purred as I rolled him under me. Once on his stomach, I pulled the cheeks of his firm ass apart. I growled loudly as I saw his pink hole, knowing I would be the first to breach it. "This ass is mine now!"

"Shit! Ty, wait until you feel this." Cord hissed out as I licked over his hole. I did it slowly several times before pushing my tongue inside of him. Cord screamed out my name as his cock exploded, the muscles in his ass clamping down on my tongue. I didn't stop. I kept rimming his ass as he came hard. "It's too much, baby. I can't take anymore."

"I've got you, Cord," I said gently as I pulled out my tongue and ran my claws down his back. I was very careful not to scratch him. "It's going to be extremely intense, but you'll get used to it. You'll probably pass out the first few times."

"How are you going to stretch him out with claws?" Ty asked from my right, holding the bottle of lube.

"That's why I have two mates." I purred as I licked along Cord's back. "I can calm down a bit if someone gives me some relief. That should give you enough time to stretch each other out."

"Come up here, baby," Cord panted as he pushed up off the bed. "I'll suck on that wonderful dick of yours while Ty gets me ready. If that's okay with you, Ty?"

"My pleasure." Ty chuckled as he took my place behind Cord.

"You don't have to do this already," I said apprehensively as I moved around to Cord's head. "I know this is your first time with a man. You don't have to suck me off."

"I want to," he replied, smiling up at me as he got on his hands and knees. "It felt amazing to me when you did it last night. I want to try it. Besides, you just took me to heaven when you ate my ass. I want to make you feel good, too."

"You're so amazing," I whispered as I leaned down and kissed him. I kept my mouth closed and gave him just a quick peck, knowing my razor sharp teeth could slice his tongue up into bits. I lined up my cock with his mouth and just held it there for him to explore. He winked at me before licking the head. I moaned at the feeling as I got a front row seat to Ty preparing Cord for me.

"That's so hot." Ty groaned as he watched Cord suck on my dick. He pushed one then two fingers in Cord's ass, realizing I'd already opened him up a bit with my tongue. When Cord swallowed down over half my cock, I couldn't keep my hips still and thrust forward.

"Sorry," I said pulling back when he started choking. "It just felt so good."

"I'm doing okay then?" Cord asked after he pulled his mouth off my dick. His eyes stared into mine, his insecurities completely apparent.

"It felt amazing," I answered, running my claws through his hair.

"Ty, I need more." Cord groaned, pushing back on Ty's hand.

"I've got three fingers in you," Ty answered, shrugging at me.

"I know what you need, Cord," I said, giving him a feral smile. I crawled to the other side of the bed and pulled Ty's fingers out of his ass. Cord bemoaned the loss, but I immediately replaced the fingers with my cock. "You're so fucking tight."

"I feel so full." Cord hissed, looking at me over his shoulder. "Is it always like this?"

"Yes," I grunted, trying to slowly work my cock deeper into him. I wanted nothing more to thrust into him hard and bottom out, but I wouldn't risk hurting him.

"I need more, Avery," he begged as he lowered his shoulders to the bed. Ty moved to kneel at the front of the bed as he poured some more lube on his fingers. I growled my approval as he pushed a finger into his own ass.

"Oh, you like seeing me stretch myself out for you, don't you baby?" Ty asked, knowing the answer.

"More than you know." I purred as I pushed in the last two inches into Cord. We both moaned loudly when I was all the way in. I licked along his back, my eyes never leaving Ty as I gave Cord time to adjust to my dick. "Tell me when you're ready, Cord."

"The burning's passed," Cord panted. "I kind of liked it, though."

"Just wait until I bite you." I snickered as I slowly pulled out of him until only the head of my cock remained in him. Thrusting forward, I slammed my dick right back into him.

"Harder, Avery," he moaned, and I took him at his word. Leaning forward over his back, I licked his neck as I started to pound into his ass. "So fucking good."

"Mine," I growled, running my sharp teeth over his neck. Cord shivered under me. "You're mine and Ty's now, Cord. I will rip anyone to shreds who tries to touch you or take what is mine."

"Possessive bastard." Ty chuckled. I saw he had two fingers in his ass then. "Are you always this dominant?"

"Not even close," I panted as I fucked Cord with everything I had. "Normally, I'm a bottom, but claiming my mates is bringing out the Alpha in me."

"Do it, bite me, make me yours," Cord whimpered as he submissively tilted his head. I felt a thrill go through me as I saw my mate giving me what I wanted. Leaning down, I was about to bite him when I realized something.

"Fuck!" I screamed as I stopped what I was doing.

"What?" They both yelled.

"I forgot to tell you something," I panted, pissed I was ruining the moment. "The marks will heal but never fully go away."

"I'll have a scar?" Cord asked, exchanging a look with Ty.

"Kinda, but it will become a hot spot," I answered, realizing how badly I'd screwed up. "It won't be very big, but every month I'll reclaim you there. It won't hurt, just look like a healed bite mark."

"Thank you for warning me," Cord said, smiling at me over his shoulder. "Now fuck me and claim me."

"Are you sure?" I asked.

"A little scar that will become an erogenous zone for me won't stop me from keeping you, Avery," he answered gently. "I'm already falling for you, and I've loved Ty for years. You're like the glue that's going to hold us all together."

"Thank you," I whispered, leaning forward and giving him a quick peck again.

"You're welcome. Now fuck me," Cord purred. "It felt more amazing than any sex I've ever had before."

"You'd better love it. You're going to get it like this at least three times a month." I chuckled as I moved my hips around.

"Bring it on." He moaned. I glanced at Ty, who gave me a nod, before thrusting forward again. Grabbing his shoulders gently, I changed the angle to hit Cord's prostate on every thrust. "Oh, fuck, don't stop. Whatever you're doing, please don't stop ever."

"I'm going to come just from watching you two." Ty hissed as he stroked his dick. He had three fingers in his ass now as he played with himself.

"Go ahead, but you'll come again when I take your ass next." I growled. Leaning back down, I licked Cord's neck and shoulder. Right when I felt him stiffen up, I sank my canines into his left shoulder. He screamed loudly as he climaxed, shooting his spunk all over the bed. The muscles in his ass massaged my cock as I kept pounding into him. Raising my head, I let out a roar that shook the windows. I grabbed his hips and fucked him like a madman as I came. Just as I was finishing, the knot in my cock extended and latched onto Cord's prostate.

"Holy shit, what is that?" Cord screamed as he climaxed again.

"I forgot about that." I moaned as I kept moving my hips around. I couldn't go far while I was attached to him, but Cord was going nuts under me as I did it. "It only happens with true mates."

"What? What happens?" Ty asked, his eyes darting from me then back to Cord.

"Something latched onto my prostate," Cord cried out. Then he collapsed under me. I moved my hands in time to hold my weight so I didn't fall on him.

"You fucked him into passing out." Ty chuckled, and I saw he'd removed his fingers from his ass. "I'm so going to give him shit that he blacked out."

"You're next," I growled as the knot receded. I groaned as I pulled out of Cord's ass, my cock still rock hard.

"I am, am I?" Ty snickered, and I froze.

"You changed your mind?" I whispered, feeling as if my heart was breaking.

"No, I was just teasing, Avery," he said as he moved toward me. He pulled me into his arms and held me tight. "I want you to be mine as I will be yours."

"Sorry, I don't seem to get all of your jokes." I sighed as I laid my head on his shoulder. I felt relieved when I realized he still wanted me.

"You will. It will just take some time," Ty replied gently. When he moved, I got a good look at where I'd be claiming him and growled. "What's wrong?"

"Nothing. I need to bite you now." I snarled. In a flash, I got off the bed, pulled him to the edge, and bent him over.

"Shit, you're strong." He gasped. I smiled as I lined up my cock and started to push into him. "Oh, fuck, it burns!"

"Sorry, I can go slower," I said, stopping what I was doing.

"Don't you dare, I love it." He moaned. "Oh, shit, fuck me, baby."

"Gladly," I growled as I slammed back into him. His ass was like snug, tight heaven. It molded and caressed my cock as I thrust in and out of him.

"I've been craving this all my life." Ty hissed. "Give me everything you got, Avery. Pound my ass raw."

"I had no idea that you were this kinky." I purred as I licked along his back.

"I didn't either," he panted as his hands fisted in the sheets. "It just feels so fucking good. I want more."

I pistoned into his ass like an animal, no pun intended. When I felt him getting close, I leaned over and licked his right shoulder. "Are you ready, my mate?"

"Yes, bite me, Avery." Ty moaned, pushing back on my cock. I sunk my teeth into his soft flesh. He screamed as he climaxed, his ass muscles tightening around my dick. I drank his life force down then lifted my head and roared out my orgasm. His ass milked my cock, drawing every last drop of cum out of me before my knot extended and latched onto him. "Oh, fuck, that's what Cord was talking about."

"You like that, Ty?" I hissed as I kept thrusting in and out of him as much as I could.

"It's nirvana." He groaned before collapsing over the side of the bed. Seconds later, the knot went back into my cock, and I fell to the side of Ty. Glancing around, I laughed at my two very large mates passed out on the bed. I felt kind of bad that they were just passed out in their own cum. Getting up, I went into the bathroom and got some warm washcloths. I went back to them and got them all cleaned up.

Then I went over to Cord, picked him up, pulled up the sheets, and laid him back down. I did the same for Ty, making sure that they were lying comfortable on their backs. Staring at them, I felt my heart fill with love for my newly claimed mates. As I went to lie in between them, my body started to heat up. I realized I was going into honeymoon heat.

I shifted back to human form, crawled over to the nightstand, and grabbed the lube. Squirting some on my fingers, I inserted one in my ass as I leaned over and took Cord's semi-hard dick in my mouth. He moaned in his sleep, his cock growing in my mouth. Quickly stretching myself, I pushed in another finger, then a third.

"Can I always wake up this way?" Cord groaned. I smiled up at him, pulling my fingers from my ass and moving to straddle him. His eyes got wide with lust as I grabbed his cock and slowly lowered myself onto him. "Oh, baby, you're so tight."

"Glad you like because the heat already started." I hissed as he bottomed out inside me. "I want to be on the bottom."

"Whatever my baby wants." He chuckled as he rolled us over. I wrapped my arms and legs around him as he started to fuck me.

"Oh, crap, can I always wake up this way?" Ty moaned. I shared a look with Cord then we burst out laughing. Ty stared at us like we'd lost it. "What's so funny?"

"I said the same thing when I came around and Avery was sucking my cock," Cord answered. He stared into my eyes as he slowly pulled out of me before thrusting back in. "Now, I'm going to give our baby as much of the bliss he gave us that I can."

"You act like I didn't enjoy it, as well." I purred as I leaned up and licked my mating marks on his shoulder.

"I take it sex-a-palooza's started?" Ty chuckled.

"Yeah, I'm in honeymoon heat." I moaned as Cord started to pick up the pace. "It's going to be a few days of naked fun."

"Bring it on." Cord smirked before mashing his lips down on mine.

Chapter 4

A couple days later, the honeymoon heat was over. I woke up alone and sore in all the right places. Crawling out of bed, I stood up and waddled almost completely bowlegged out of the room. I giggled as I got to the top of the stairs, loving every tight muscle and every pain I felt, smiling at how I got it. Halfway down the stairs, a smell hit my nose.

"Wolf," I snarled as I leapt down the rest of the stairs, shifting mid leap. Barreling through the living room to the kitchen, I immediately put myself in between my mates and the stranger. Snarling loudly, I got low, ready to pounce, giving every clue I could that I wasn't fucking around.

"Avery, stop, it's just Frank," Cord said, stepping in front of me. I was about to push him out of the way when there was a loud growl from behind him. Cord's eyes went wide as he slowly turned to look over his shoulder, like out of a horror movie. "Frank? What the fuck, man?"

"He's a werewolf." I snarled after I'd shifted into my half and half form, seeing Frank already had claws and huge teeth. Being an over four hundred pound tiger wouldn't give me the mobility I'd need if a fight broke out in the house. I grabbed Cord and pushed him behind me with Ty. "What do you want with my mates?"

"Your mates?" The werewolf gasped. "I'm going to shift back. I'm not a threat. I'm friends with Cord and Ty. They called me here, tiger."

"You shift to human, and I will." I nodded, hoping it was just a misunderstanding. I watched as he shifted to human, and I was about to do the same.

"Actually, can you shift back to tiger?" he asked gently. I raised an eyebrow at him and let the change over take me. He knelt down in front of me on one knee. "I thought sabers were just a legend. I've met other weretigers, but seeing you is almost surreal."

"No touching our mate," Ty said as he stepped in between Frank and me. I shifted back chuckling, stood, and plastered my body to Ty's back.

"I love it when you get all possessive." I giggled. He wrapped his arms back around me, touching my naked skin.

"You really need to start dressing, baby," Cord grumbled. I looked over my shoulder to see him whip off his shirt then pull it over my head. Snickering, I pulled it on the rest of the way, putting my arms through the holes. Cord was so much bigger than I was that I was swimming in his shirt. "So, you're a werewolf, Frank."

"Um, yeah. So you mated a saber, Cord." Frank snickered.

"All right, let's have some coffee," Ty replied, wiping his hands over his face. "It's obvious we need to talk."

"Feed me. I'm hungry." I pouted. "After days of carnal pleasures, I'm starved."

"What are you in the mood for, baby?" Cord chuckled as he went to the fridge.

"Can you make me that sandwich again?" I purred, rubbing myself on the side of his body. "That was so yummy."

"Avery, that's all you've eaten since you've gotten here," Ty said gently. "There are other foods to eat. Maybe it's time to try something else."

"Okay." I shrugged as I sat at the kitchen table. "As long as it's not raw meat."

"Deal," Cord replied, giving me a wink. "I think I have something that you'll love."

"You guys are too good to me," I answered, giving him air kisses.

"Have a seat, Frank," Ty said as he grabbed the pot of coffee and some cups. Frank and Ty both sat down as Ty poured the coffee and Cord started mixing something in a bowl. We all just stared at each other for several minutes as we fixed our coffee the way we liked it. I found out that I really liked it with lots of sugar and a little milk, not cream.

"Too bad I trashed another uniform," Frank finally said, breaking the silence. He pulled on his shirt, and sure enough most of the seams were ripped. "Good think the other deputies and sheriff are werewolves, too."

"I didn't know there was a local pack, or I would have come to tell you I was on your land," I replied quietly. "There are extenuating circumstances."

"I'll pass that along." Frank nodded. "But you know our Alpha will want to talk with you."

"I understand, but I ask that we keep this from your council for the time being," I said. "And I don't want Ty and Cord brought into this."

"Yes to the first. I'm not sure on the second," Frank replied, giving me a pitied look. "Does your council know that you're here?"

"Stop this!" Cord yelled, slamming down a skillet. He spun around and gestured widely. "What are you guys even talking about? Councils and secret handshakes? You've been our friend for over a decade, Frank. How could you keep this from us?"

I got up quickly and stood in front of Cord, putting my hands on his chest. "I'm sorry. We'll explain this. Don't be mad at Frank. His pack would have ordered him to keep it secret. I've told you how some humans handle the news of shifters. They can't risk that type of exposure. I know this is confusing, and I'll tell you everything. But please, Cord, I need you to be strong for me, okay? I need you and Ty to be my rock and support me."

"Okay, baby," he said after taking several deep breaths. I stood up on my tiptoes and gave him a quick kiss before going back to my seat.

"Let's start at the beginning, Frank." I smiled at him and gave Ty a wink.

"Fair enough," Frank answered. "I'm assuming, then, your mates no nothing of our ways?"

"No, I showed up on their doorstep injured, dumped our existence on them, and we mated," I explained, twisting my hands together. "And then I went into honeymoon heat. This is the day after it, and here you are."

"That honeymoon heat is real?" he asked, his eyes going wide with a smirk on his face.

"Yeah, lunar cycle affects all shifters differently." I giggled then explained our ways of mating. "Cord, Ty, there are a lot more werewolves than weretigers, especially on this continent. They live in packs with an Alpha as leader and Betas as, like, their enforcers. All weres have their own councils, along with vampires and pretty much every supernatural being."

"We don't cross over into other were's territory without permission from the locals," Frank said, picking up my explanation. "Weres have their own set of rules and laws."

"And by me breaking that rule, my life is forfeit," I replied gently, watching Cord and Ty.

"No fucking way. They aren't getting you," Ty yelled, jumping out of his seat. "Frank, you can't let them take Avery. He didn't know there were werewolves around here!"

"Your pack is not taking our mate," Cord screamed, throwing his mug of coffee at the wall.

"Wait!" Frank shouted, holding up his hands to my mates. "Avery, those haven't been the laws in a long time. You should know that."

"They haven't?" I asked, completely shocked. "I didn't know that they changed."

"How could you not know that?" Frank replied, his eyebrows scrunching.

"He's been in captivity for almost thirty years," Ty answered, coming to me and gathering me up in his arms. "Some hunters took him from his family when he was a boy and kept him in some freak-show circus."

"Were there other weres there?" Frank asked.

"Yeah, there was a wolf, a couple of merfolk, and other shifters I never saw," I answered quietly. "They kept us all separate so we couldn't gang up on them."

"I would call that an extenuating circumstance," Frank replied, wiping his hands over his face. "I need to make a call."

"Avery's not in danger, right?" Cord asked, grabbing Frank's arm as he stood up.

"No, my Alpha is a good man. He won't hurt Avery," Frank answered gently before leaving the room.

"I'm so sorry," I whispered, feeling overwhelming despair for what I'd dragged my mates into.

"This isn't your fault, baby," Ty replied, kissing the top of my head. I wrapped my arms around his waist, needing to feel him. Cord came up behind me and hugged both of us. I glanced up just in time to see them kiss.

"Damn, that's hot." I hissed, rubbing against both of them. "I think we should all get naked after breakfast."

"Dirty, dirty little mate." Cord chuckled as he leaned down and licked my neck. "But we need to get you fed then deal with the wolves. And Ty needs to go feed the horses."

"No starting without me." Ty groaned and adjusted his groin before moving away from us and heading out the back door.

"We'll figure this all out, okay, baby?" Cord whispered in my ear, hugging me from behind.

"I know," I replied, melting into his embrace. He smacked my ass, and I groaned. "Do it again."

"You liked that?" He hissed, pushing his hard, jeans-covered cock into my lower back. "I think Ty and I are going to have some fun punishing our little mate."

"What did I do wrong?" I gasped as I spun in his arms. "Whatever I did, I'm sorry. Please don't punish me!"

"Avery, sweetheart, I was just teasing," Cord said gently as he wiped away the tear that fell down my cheek. "We're not really going to punish you. I was just playing because you liked me spanking you."

"Oh, thank god," I whispered, burying my face in his chest. "I can't take anymore cages or whips."

"No, we would never do that to you, baby," he replied, rubbing my back. "But bad little mates get spanked for their punishments."

I turned my head and gazed up at him as he waggled his eyebrows at me. The light bulb went off over my head then. "Oh, I get it. It's not really punishment if I enjoy it, and I don't really have to be bad."

"Exactly." He chuckled. His hands roamed under his shirt I was wearing, landing on my ass and squeezing it firmly. "I want in this hot little ass as soon as Frank's gone."

"But, for right now, Frank can hear you." Frank snickered from behind us. "Man, you didn't just finally come out of the closet, Cord. You leaped out and hooked two men."

"You knew?" Cord asked, stiffening up and removing his hands from me.

"Everyone knew, Cord," Frank replied gently as we walked back toward the table. Cord went back to mixing something in the bowl. I couldn't help but stare at his muscular back as he moved. "You and Ty shared something special, even back in high school. No one cared, man. We all wanted you to be happy."

"I am now," he said, winking at me over his shoulder. "Avery's hot little body was too much to resist. He made us own up to how Ty and I really felt about each other."

"And we will forever love him for that," Ty added from the doorway.

"You what?" I gasped, almost dropping my coffee cup.

"We love you, Avery," Cord said firmly as he turned to face us. "How could we not? You're so amazing, baby. From the moment you showed up here, you've done nothing but show us love and affection. Today, you jumped in front of us to protect us without a single thought of the danger you might be getting into. But you didn't care. That's just who you are, your heart right on your sleeve."

"Thank you," I whispered, tears filling up my eyes as I looked from one of my men to the other. "I love you both, too."

"Then we have everything we need," Ty said as he came and whipped me up into his arms. As always, I immediately wrapped my arms and legs around him, needing to feel as much of him as possible. "Frank, you need to leave now. We're going to make love to our little tiger."

"We need to talk first," Frank replied, clearing his throat, obviously uncomfortable. "My Alpha is on his way to talk to Avery."

"Is he in trouble?" Ty asked, turning as if to protect me from some perceived threat.

"No, I explained there was a lot more than just an unknown shifter showing up," Frank answered, shaking his head. "He just wants to talk and get the story from the source. More than likely, the pack will step up and help keep your mate safe."

"You can trust Frank, baby," Cord whispered in my ear as he set down a plate of pancakes in front of me. Ty set me down on my feet as I took my chair again. "We've known him since we were kids. And while him being a werewolf is news, he's still a good guy that I'd trust with my life."

"Thanks, Cord," Frank replied, chuckling when Cord jumped. "We have really good hearing."

"You'll get used to it, big guy." I giggled as I picked up a fork. "These look amazing. I've not had pancakes since I was a kid."

As I started cutting into my food, I realized the room got quiet. Stuffing my face, I looked up and saw Ty and Cord watching me with tears in their eyes.

"It's okay, guys," I said quietly. "I'm free now and with people who love me. I can't change what happened to me, simply move on from it."

"You really are amazing, Avery," Ty replied as he sat down next to me. "Most people wouldn't have that attitude after going through what happened to you."

"I've got too much to be grateful for to focus on that shit," I answered, smiling widely at him. I ate another mouthful of the pancakes, moaning in delight. It was like eating warm, buttery bliss. "And I'll do anything you want to get pancakes made for me every so often."

"Anything, huh?" Cord snickered, wiggling his eyebrows at me. "I'll hold you to that."

Before I could even respond, the doorbell rang. Frank gave Ty a nod, and he went to answer it. I ate up my food as quickly as I could, knowing it would be rude to eat in front of strangers.

"Pastor Daniels? You're the pack's Alpha? You've gotta be shitting me," Ty exclaimed from the foyer. Cord's jaw just about hit the floor as Frank just sat there smiling widely, sipping his coffee. "Sorry, Pastor, come on in."

"Thanks, Ty." A deep voice chuckled. They got to the kitchen just as I was swallowing my last bite of pancakes. A tall, lean, older man followed Ty into the kitchen. He had Alpha written all over him. In a flash, I got out of my chair and kneeled at his feet, baring the back of my neck to him.

"Alpha, forgive me for entering your territory," I said formally. The man laughed, scaring the crap out of me. I wasn't expecting that response.

"It's all right, little one," Pastor Daniels said as he took my hand to get me to stand up. "I hear there's a reason for it."

"Yes, Alpha," I replied, breathing a sigh of relief when he gestured for me to sit back down.

"Cord, Ty, I take it you've been told about our world and why it's so important you keep all of this secret," the Alpha said as he took a chair opposite me. Cord and Ty nodded as they took chairs on either side of me. Frank had gotten up when the Alpha had come in, out of respect. But now he took a seat at his Alpha's left. "Tell me everything, tiger."

"My name is Avery Donovan," I replied after taking a deep breath. And then I explained everything, my kidnapping, the years in captivity, and how I ended up on Ty and Cord's doorstep. The entire time, each of my mates held one of my hands in support. Cord took over the story from there—how they found me shot, revealing what I was to them and our mating. Well, not *all* about our mating, just that it happened and the honeymoon heat.

The Alpha sat there in silence, taking it all in as he eyed me over. When Cord was finally done, we sat there in silence for several moments before the Alpha spoke. "You wouldn't be Martin Donovan's boy, would you?"

"You know my dad?" I answered, realizing that I'd answered his question with a question.

"I do," he nodded solemnly. "Your family has been looking for you since the moment you were taken. He checks in with all the packs and shifter leaders every few months to see if anyone has heard anything about you."

"Do you know how to contact him?" I gasped, completely shocked as to the turn this conversation was taking.

"I do," the Alpha said smiling warmly. He pulled out a cell phone and punched in some numbers. We all waited on pins and needles. "Martin, it's Chester Daniels. I have someone here who wants to speak with you."

I stared at him, tears falling freely now as he handed me his phone. "Dad?"

"Oh, my god. Avery? Is that you, son?" My father cried out on the other line.

"Yes, it's me," I sobbed, trying to wipe away my tears. Cord pulled me onto his lap and hugged me tightly. "I've missed you all so much! Is everyone okay? Was anyone else hurt or taken?"

"No, only you, my baby boy," my father cried. "I'm so sorry I couldn't protect you, Avery."

"Avery? Avery, are you there?" My mother whispered as she got on the line. "Are you all right?"

"Yes, Mom, I'm fine now," I answered. "I escaped and found my mates."

"Oh, thank the heavens." She gasped. "Where are you? We're coming to you immediately."

"I'm in Montana, in Alpha Daniels' pack territory," I said, glancing to Ty and Cord, asking for permission to give them the address. They both nodded, tears flowing down their cheeks, as well. I gave my mother the exact address that I read from an envelope Cord handed me.

"We're not far. We'll be there within two hours," my mother replied. "I love you, Avery. I've prayed every night for your safe return."

"I know, Mom," I whispered. "Tell Dad it's not his fault. It's no one's fault but the hunters."

"I'll kill them all." My father growled in the background. "We'll hunt those fuckers down and rip them to shreds."

"Are my brothers coming, too?" I asked, completely touched by father's words.

"Yes, they all live close. We'll pick them up on the way," my mother answered. "We love you, son."

"I love you, too. See you soon," I replied as we hung up. I handed the phone back to Alpha Daniels. "Thank you so much."

"I had a child taken by hunters some years back," the Alpha said gently. "She didn't survive it. No parent should ever have to bear losing a child."

I nodded, completely understanding, before turning and burying my head in Cord's neck. I cried out all my years of grief and worry that my family was killed by the hunters. Ty moved into my chair and hugged me from behind. I heard them sniffling even through my sobs.

"It's okay now, baby," Cord cooed. "Your family's safe. No one else was taken."

"How did you know that's why I was crying?" I asked, raising my head to look at him.

"Because it's you, Avery," Ty answered as if that explained everything. "You wouldn't be crying because of what happened to you. You worry about everyone else first."

"I have an idea," Cord said, taking my face in his hands. "Your parents will be here in a few hours, right?" I nodded, and he winked at Ty over my shoulder. "Let's do some shopping and get you some clothes because I get cranky when others see that sexy body of yours. And we can pick up a bunch of food and throw a party."

"I think that's a great idea," Ty replied, turning toward Alpha Daniels. "I know we're mated to a different type of shifter and all, but I figure we're, like, distant cousins with the wolves now. It's incredibly last minute, but we'd be honored if anyone from the pack would like to join us. I think it'd be a great way to get to know your crew, celebrate our mating and Avery's reunion with his family."

"Almost like a wedding reception," the Alpha agreed, smiling widely. "I'll see who is available, but we're grateful to be included."

"You found our baby's parents," Cord replied quietly. "We're indebted to you. If you ever need anything, please just ask."

"Cord, I don't have money for any of this," I whispered in his ear.

"Yeah, like you have to worry about that with these guys." Frank chuckled. "They're loaded."

"You are?" I asked, completely shocked.

"We told you that you don't have to worry about money, Avery," Ty answered. "Besides the ranch my family let us, Cord's parents left him several coal mines they owned in Wyoming."

"I landed two sugar daddies?" I giggled, squirming on Cord's lap. "Go me!"

"Come on. We've got a lot to get done." Cord chuckled as he held my hips in place. "Sex can be later."

"We'll get out of your hair." Alpha Daniels snickered. "It's after one now, so I'll tell everyone anytime after four. That should give you all time to reunite in private."

"Thank you for everything you've done, Alpha," I said as I got off Cord's lap and hugged the man. "For understanding why I'm here and not being pissed, but mostly for calling my dad."

"When Frank called to tell me we had a saber here that had been in captivity, I hoped that it would be you," he replied as he stood and pulled away. "I've known your dad for a long time, and I've prayed for the day you could find each other. I'm glad I could help."

"We won't forget it, Pastor Daniels," Ty said as he extended his hand to the man. "Or do we call you Alpha, too?"

"When we're among my pack or shifters, Alpha." He chuckled. "When other humans are around, Pastor is fine. I'm both."

"Thanks, Frank." Cord patted the man on the shoulder. "You're a good friend."

"I'm just glad you guys are happy." He snickered as we walked them to the door. "We'll see you guys later."

We said the rest of our goodbyes and closed the door behind them. Then Cord turned and glanced at me with an evil look in his eyes. "Now, about this spanking you like?"

"He likes to be spanked?" Ty asked, eyes going wide. "That's totally turning me on."

"Oh, shit." I giggled as I raced up the stairs and to our room. We'd decided that Cord's room would be our room since it was bigger. The new bed should be coming tomorrow, and I couldn't wait to test it out. I barely got to the bathroom when I saw they were in the room, too. They looked at each other and then at me, obviously freaked at how fast they could run now. "Cool, isn't it?"

"Yeah, but freaky, too," Ty answered. "I noticed it early when I was feeding the horses. Things that were normally heavy to me aren't anymore."

"You're not mad, are you?" I asked hesitantly as I walked toward them. "I know it's going to take some getting used to, but don't be pissed, okay?"

"We're not upset, Avery." He chuckled as he gave me a quick peck. Cord did the same before they dug through the dressers and found some clothes I didn't completely swim in. Once we were ready, we all walked out the door and climbed into the truck. I was sitting between my two hot, incredibly loving men, and it just felt like exactly where I belonged.

Chapter 5

"Seriously, you guys are spending way too much money," I whined as Ty added *more* clothes to our shopping cart. It wasn't like we were at some high-end retail store. We were at Old Navy. I'd at least talked Ty into going there instead of Abercrombie & Fitch like he'd wanted to while Cord ran to the liquor store. Luckily, Billings, Montana, was less than a half an hour away from the little town we lived in.

"Just be glad we don't have time to go to the adult store." Ty chuckled as we went to the register. He'd filled the cart in less than fifteen minutes since we were on a tight timeline. Cord was going to pick us up out front, and we were going to hit a place called Costco. I wasn't really sure what it was, but my men told me I'd love it.

"Ty, put some of that back." I hissed as I saw the total hit over five hundred, and the lady had only rung up about half of the items.

"Now I do have a reason to spank you later," Ty whispered in my ear. "I *want* to do this, Avery. Don't deprive me of having fun spoiling my mate."

"Fine." I giggled, all annoyance leaving me when he stuck out his lower lip in a pout. Ty paid for everything, and we grabbed the bags before heading out the door.

"That's not nearly enough clothes for Avery," Cord said as we got in the truck.

"We're on a time crunch here," Ty replied, shooting Cord a look. "We *can* come back."

"Fair enough." Cord snickered as he drove toward the next place. "I think we need to hit up the adult store next trip."

"Great minds think alike." I laughed. "Ty said the same thing in Old Navy."

"Nice," Cord replied as he bumped fists with Ty. "I was thinking a remote control plug we could use on you, baby."

"Oh, do tell," I purred as I slid my hand in between his thighs. He gave a cute yelp in shock as he pulled into a parking lot. I glanced out the window and saw a *huge* store. "What is this place?"

"It's a wholesale store. A little of everything, but in bulk," Ty answered as we all got out of the truck. I took his hand, feeling like a little kid as we walked to the doors of the gigantic store. It was like a tiny mall in itself. Cord grabbed us a cart and showed the woman at the door something like a driver's license.

"Holy shit." I gasped as we walked about twenty feet into the store. There was a huge electronics department on the right and all kinds of goodies on the left. I walked with my mouth open as Ty and Cord led me toward the back. Once we got to the food department, I saw a woman handing out samples. "Can I try one?"

"You don't have to ask us, Avery." Cord snickered. He was loading up the cart with buns before moving and grabbing tons of meat to grill. As we went, I tried every sample I could get my hands on.

"We so have to get some of this." I moaned after eating some cheesecake. "I want to just bathe in this."

"Only if we get to lick it off you," Ty whispered in my ear, causing me to burst into peals of laughter. Cord simply winked at me as he added two to our cart. I was so amazed with the store. There was everything you could think of. There was even a huge walk-in refrigerator that had all types of fruits and vegetables. I stared as Cord and Ty loaded up the bottom of the cart with all types of party trays.

"This is going to cost a fortune," I grumbled.

"Cheaper than a wedding reception," Cord chuckled as he let Ty push the cart and threw an arm over my shoulder. "It gives us an excuse to throw a party. I can't remember the last time Ty and I even had people over."

"Yeah, we're normally reclusive." Ty chuckled. "I think we need another cart."

"I'd say so," Cord answered. "Okay, you get the hard liquor, chips, dip, condiments, and grilling veggies. Oh, and some non-beer bottles of booze."

"On it." Ty saluted before sprinting toward the front of the store.

"I love you," I said solemnly, touched by how much they loved spoiling me.

"I love you, too, baby," he replied, leaning down to give me a kiss.

"I don't need to see that shit," a man near us sneered. "This is a family store."

"And I still have my clothes on, so shut your trap." I snarled at him. I must have been better at it than a normal human would because the guy's eyes went wide, and he booked it. I turned back to Cord, my cheeks heating up. "Sorry."

"I thought it was hot." He snickered as he pulled me close to him. I laughed as he moved me in between his arms as he pushed the cart. We kept walking along. I just smiled as Cord put more and more into the cart. Finally, we made our way back up front where Ty met us with an impish grin on his face. Cord went in his pocket and took out his keys, tossing them to me. "Why don't you pull up the truck, Avery?"

I just stared at the keys, feeling like a complete schmuck. Before I could even remind them I didn't know how to drive nor had a license, they both were by me and hugged me fiercely.

"I'm such a dumbass. Can you forgive me, baby?" Cord asked gently.

"Nothing to forgive," I answered, pulling away when I saw everyone was staring. "Maybe you can teach me to drive so we don't have it come up again?"

"No way. Cord sucks." Ty snickered, seeing I was uncomfortable. "I'll teach you to drive."

I rolled my eyes at him, laughing, and that was all it took to break the tension. Knowing it was going to be bad, I didn't even look to see what the total was. As we loaded back up the cart, Ty and I talked about how the value wasn't the same as it was the last time I went shopping. The cashier gave us a look like we'd lost it, but she had no clue it'd been thirty years.

We got everything loaded up and back home in less than twenty-five minutes. Cord had been speeding, saying we were getting too close to the two-hour mark. Once home, we started unloading the completely packed bed of the truck. On my third trip out, I saw a blue SUV coming up the drive. I knew who it was and froze, completely overwhelmed with emotions.

"Avery!" my mom shouted as she jumped from the car before it had even fully stopped. I dropped the bags and raced to her.

"Mom," I gasped as I pulled her into my arms. We were squeezing each other so tightly it was any wonder either of us could breathe.

"Son," my dad Beck, whispered as he hugged me and mom. "We've missed you so."

"Me, too," I hiccupped, tears falling freely. "I thought this day would never come."

"You're safe," she replied, her body shaking with sobs. My other father, Martin, joined in the hug. Just then, I heard several growls. Glancing in that direction, I saw my older brothers flanking us.

"Guys, back off. They're my mates." I chuckled, wiping the tears from my eyes. I dislodged myself from my parents' arms and went to stand by my men. "This is Cord Hartwell and Tyson Fitzgerald. Cord, Ty, these are my parents, Martin, Beck, and Ashley Donovan."

"It's so nice to meet you both," my mother said, coming to hug them both. "Thank you for taking such good care of my boy."

"It's our pleasure." Ty chuckled, but Cord stiffened up and moved out of the way.

"Cord?" I asked, concerned at his odd reaction.

"I'm sorry. It's just been so long since I've had a mom hug," Cord whispered. His eyes were wide and darting around, almost as if frightened.

"Cord's family was killed when he was a child," Ty explained as he wrapped an arm around Cord's waist.

"Then I think you're overdue, son," my mom said gently. She held up her hand when Cord went to argue. "You've mated my boy. That makes us family. I won't be your mother or replace her, but I am your mother-in-law."

"I guess," Cord answered quietly. I'd never seen this side of him, insecure and unsure of himself. It seemed that every big, strong guy had issues like the rest of us. My mom went to him slowly, wrapping her arms around his neck and pulling him down to her. She was pretty tall for a woman, but my mates still towered over her. Cord was stiff at first then slowly melted into the embrace and returning it.

I was just about to say something when I felt my legs get knocked out from under me. Turning my head before we hit the ground, I saw my brothers attacking me. We all laughed as the six of us wrestled and rolled in the dirt.

"I'd be getting jealous if I couldn't tell you were all related," Ty grumbled. It was true. Though we varied in size, we all had our orange-ish hair and green eyes.

"Sorry, big guy." I giggled as we started to get up. "Welcome to being a cat. We all wrestle and are very touchy-feely."

"We've noticed." Cord snorted as he moved away from my mom and went to shake my dads' hands. "Do we get names?"

"Sorry, I was just so excited to see everyone," I answered, my face heating up. I turned so I could point out the right brother. "This is Trey, Sasha, Quinn, Kody, and Jace."

"Don't take this the wrong way, baby," Ty said slowly, and I knew what was coming. "I mean, some of your brothers are my size."

"Every litter has a runt." I giggled, walking toward him. "Why? Do you wish I was bigger?"

"Hell no, I love my little mate." He growled, grabbing me up under my arms and holding me fiercely. I draped my arms and legs over him, laughing at how possessive he was. "Wait, did you just say litter? As in your mom popped out six boys in one shot?"

"Yes, I did." My mother laughed, taking my dads' hands. "And this was before they had nifty drugs to give a woman in birth."

"Dear god, woman!" Cord gasped, taking my mother's arm. "They better treat you like a goddess. I think I need a drink on your behalf!"

"Boys, help unload the grocery store in the back of their truck." My dad Martin chuckled, pointing to all our purchases. "Rob a bank, did we?"

"Avery didn't have any clothes," Cord replied gently. "So we picked him up some basics. And we knew we'd be having company, plus we invited the local pack over for a barbeque later."

"We can pay for our own way," Beck said as we walked toward the house. I was still hanging onto the front of Ty like a monkey. It really was my favorite place to be with either of my mates. I felt so loved and safe when they held me this way.

"I have no doubt of that, but you're guests at our house," Cord answered, raising an eyebrow. "Would you let me pay for anything if I came to your house?"

"Fair enough." My dad chuckled. "We just don't want to be an imposition, and there are a lot of us."

"And we eat a lot more than humans," Trey threw in as he took an arm load of groceries.

"And you're feeling us out to see if we can take care of Avery." Ty snickered. "Believe me, we can."

"I apologize," Martin replied gently as we walked into the house. "He's been in captivity so long. It's not like he's acclimated and can just get a job."

"We understand." Cord chuckled as he threw his arms over my dads' shoulders. "Ty and I are worth about a hundred million, Mr. Donovan. We will give him everything he's ever wanted in life."

"All I want is my mates. Screw the money." I giggled. But then it hit me what Cord had just said. I released Ty and slid down, staring up at him. "I'm sorry, did you just say million?"

"We told you we owned the ranch and few coal mines, baby," Ty said gently, reaching for me again. "Frank said we were loaded."

"Yeah, but damn." I gasped, looking from Ty to Cord.

"Dude, you landed hot, rich cowboys." Sasha snickered, punching me in the arm. "Be grateful."

"I am. I was before hearing they were loaded," I replied, staring at my men. "I don't care about the money. It's just a shock."

"Why? Because we don't eat caviar for breakfast?" Ty snickered.

"No, but the shopping at the wholesale store might have thrown me." I giggled as I went to them.

"They're smart enough men to not throw their money around and be wasteful," my mom answered for them. "Now, do you have a grill? There are going to be a *lot* of hungry mouths if you invited Alpha Daniels' pack."

"Crap, we didn't think about that," Ty said. "We just have one grill."

"We'll figure it out." Mother snickered. "Cord and Trey, get the grill started. Martin, Ty, Beck, and Sasha, pull out their coolers and go get some ice. Quinn, Kody, Jace, finish unloading the truck and start getting things opened."

"Yes ma'am," a chorus of answers came. I started laughing. Some things never changed. My mom was always the one in charge. When everyone left to do their jobs, she pulled me fiercely in her arms.

"Are you really okay now? Everyone else is gone. You can tell me the truth, Avery," she whispered in my ear.

"I really am fine now, Mom," I answered, hugging her back. "I'm sure there will be some nightmares, maybe a few flashbacks, but I'm okay."

"Our thoughts never left you, Avery," she cried, breaking my heart. "Your fathers were madmen, tearing up every shifter community for any information on you."

"I know. I was just so scared that you guys were hurt or taken," I replied, crying as well.

"No, they took my baby boy away from me." She gasped, trying to catch her breath enough to talk and cry.

"What's wrong here?" Cord asked as he entered the kitchen, racing to me. "Are you hurt, baby?"

I laughed as he started checking my body for some wound. "I'm fine, Cord. We were just having a moment."

"Oh, sorry, didn't mean to ruin it," he replied gently and started to move away. My mom and I both reached for him, dragging him in a group hug.

"I wanted to make sure Avery was really okay from everything that's happened," she whispered. "My emotions are all over the place—happy, then relieved, then sad for what he went through."

"I think that's normal, Ashley," Cord replied gently. "Avery was the one who was taken, but he wasn't the only one who suffered a great trauma."

"You are a very smart man, Cord," she said, staring into my mate's eyes. "I'm very happy you and Ty are mated to my son."

"We're the ones who are lucky," Cord answered, his eyes looking at the ground. "He's so full of life, and love, and affection. And he gives it all to us so freely, not to mention getting Ty and I to finally own up to how we felt about each other."

"I don't understand?" my mom asked as we all broke apart. I realized Trey was standing by the kitchen door awkwardly. Waving him over, he smiled widely at me before hugging me.

"I missed you, little bro," he whispered in my ear. "I'm glad you're safe now."

"Thanks, Trey," I answered, hugging him back. We broke apart and all sat down.

"Ty and I weren't gay," Cord tried to explain. "I mean, we were, but we didn't know how the other felt. So we never said anything about it. Hell, I tried dating women."

"And Avery turned you gay?" Trey asked, his eyebrows scrunched together.

"No, he made us realize that Ty and I felt the same way." Cord chuckled. "He made us jump out of the closet and into the deep end."

"Sorry," I answered, fidgeting with my hands. "I was on a time limit after I met my mates."

"Hey, don't ever be sorry for that," Cord said firmly as he yanked me off the chair and onto his lap. "Ty and I love that you don't beat around the bush and simply tell it as it is."

"Good thing." I giggled as he kissed my neck. Just to be a shit, I squirmed in his lap, loving the feel of him getting hard under me.

"Behave, baby. Your mother's right here." He growled and held my hips still.

"I remember what it was like after I mated your fathers." She snickered. "I barely walked for weeks."

"Mom!" Trey and I yelled. She winked at Cord before they both broke out laughing.

"Hey, I thought you guys were all working in here," Beck called out as he carried huge bags of ice into the kitchen. "More work, less goofing off."

"Slave driver," my mom pouted, sending him air kisses.

"At least I know where you got that look from," Cord whispered in my ear as he stood with me.

"I learned from the best." I giggled as I raced away from him. I knew exactly what that lustful look was in his eyes.

"Let's behave when we have guests, kids." Ty chuckled as he came into the kitchen, as well. We all started laughing then. It felt nice. I'd missed my family so much, and now that we'd seemed to get the tears and heartache out of the way, we were having fun.

"It's been my kitchen since Ty's ma passed. I'm not sure what to do," Cord grumbled about ten minutes later. My mother had completely taken over the kitchen and made no apologies for it.

"Help us set up tables and chairs outside," Beck offered. Martin nodded as he shot my mom a wink. I followed Cord, realizing I'd never seen the backyard. Taking a few steps out the backdoor, I froze on the porch. About twenty yards away, was an Olympic size pool.

"I love my mates!" I shouted as I yanked my shirt off over my head. I got my shorts off in a flash, as well, before racing naked and jumping into the pool. When I resurfaced, I saw a couple of my brothers doing the same before they launched themselves in my direction.

"None of you have trunks," Cord yelled as he kept covering his eyes at my brother's being naked.

"Welcome to living amongst shifters." Beck snickered as he pulled off his shirt, as well. "Naked doesn't bother us one bit."

I laughed as Cord simply stood there with his mouth hanging open as he watched three of my brothers and my dads join me. Feeling feisty, I hopped out of the pool and sauntered over to him.

"Was I not supposed to go in the pool?" I asked, batting my eyelashes at him. "I figured you'd like me all naked and wet, but if I was a bad mate, I'm ready for my punishment."

"You little tease." He growled as he pulled me into his arms and mashed his lips down onto mine.

"Why is everyone skinny dipping?" Ty gasped as he joined us on the deck. "If they didn't have swimsuits, couldn't they just wear their shorts?"

"I'm told it's a shifter thing." Cord chuckled, breaking the kiss. "You're lucky it's just your family you're naked around, otherwise I'd be paddling your ass, baby."

"Promises, promises," I purred as I walked over to Ty. The closer I got, the more his eyes heat up with lust. He dropped the cooler and reached for me. I skirted his attempt, only to be caught by Cord.

"We're going to do bad, dirty things to you later, mate." Ty groaned as he and Cord surrounded me.

"Very kinky, completely carnal things." Cord hissed as he rubbed his jeans-covered hard-on against me. Ty did the same from behind, and I started to turn into a lust-filled pile of goo.

"Why wait? Take me somewhere and fuck me now," I whimpered, jumping into Cord's arms. "Please? I've been very naughty."

"And that's why we're going to just keep teasing you." Ty hissed in my ear, kissing my neck. "You'll be so ready for us tonight you'll do anything we want. And I personally want you begging for it, preferably with my cock in your mouth."

"Oh, god," I moaned as I started to hump Cord's hips, not caring my family could see. "Please, I'll be good. Please, fuck me now."

"Nope." Cord chuckled as he gave me a chaste kiss on the lips and lowered me to my feet. Ty and Cord bumped fists as they walked back toward the kitchen to grab more coolers and drinks. I, on the other hand, turned and booked it for the pool. It wasn't the same as a cold shower but as close as I was going to get right then.

Chapter 6

The wolves started showing up about a half hour later. Alpha Daniels was great about introducing everyone after he'd taken a few minutes to talk with my dads in private. Luckily, everyone had thought to bring more lawn chairs and a few brought tables. It seemed the local pack had had their share of last-minute parties.

My dads manned the grill mostly, turning out more hotdogs, burgers, and brats than most grills do in their lifetime. Everyone laughed, joked around, and helped out wherever they could. I made sure to check on Ty and Cord as often as I could.

"We're good, baby." Cord chuckled about the tenth time I checked on him. "We've known most of these people our whole lives. We simply didn't know they were werewolves."

"Dads, Avery, we're putting together a football game, come on," Kody yelled over to us. I smiled. Man, when was the last time I'd played shifter football? Then came the sadness that always started to overwhelm me when I remembered why it had been so long since I'd done something. Shaking it off, I jogged over to Kody. I saw all my brothers, my dads, and eight wolves had gathered. "You guys play the same rules, no claws tackle?"

"Yep, that's how we roll." One wolf chuckled. I thought I'd heard his name was Kane, but I'd met so many people I couldn't be sure.

"Never mind." Ty laughed as he turned around and headed back toward the deck. "Men who don't have claws shouldn't play with those who do."

"I love when you play with me, my mate," I yelled after him. He shook his head and kept walking while I got elbowed by a couple of my brothers. "Cats versus wolves?"

"You got it, little bro," Trey answered as everyone started to get undressed. "We're letting the wolves receive first."

"Sounds like a plan." I snickered, knowing my brothers were kickass at football. Well, at least they had been. I shifted quickly, trying to keep my mind on happy thoughts.

"How is anyone going to catch the ball?" Cord asked Alpha Daniels as we all finished shifting and lining up on opposite sides of what we designated as the field.

"You'll see," the Alpha laughed. Kody took the ball in his mouth and flung it down field. It was a great toss, one of the wolves catching it instantly. Quinn and I had always been the fastest, taking off for the wolf with the ball. My brothers and dads followed, trying to keep the other wolves off of us, so we could get to their wolf with the ball. I got broadsided about ten feet away from my goal, but Quinn got through, tackling the wolf. They'd gotten about a quarter of the way down the field.

"Shit, did you see how fast our baby is?" Ty asked Cord. We all lined up again, waiting for the snap. The wolf that they'd designated as the center tossed the ball to their quarterback. A few of my brothers fought to get to him, but he was able to throw the ball before they could. I was guarding one of their receivers, who the toss was aimed at. At the last second, I bumped him out of the way, leaped up and caught the ball in my mouth. Turning in the direction of our goal, I took off.

Running as fast as I could, I ducked a few wolves as my brothers took care of a few others. Finally, it was me and one wolf guarding the end zone. Faking right and breaking left, I was able to get several feet before he figured it out. I leapt over him with ease, skidding easily into the end zone. Of course, then I spiked the ball on the ground, doing a goofy victory dance as best a saber-toothed tiger could. And I stepped on the ball.

"And that would be why we always bring several footballs to any event." Alpha Daniels laughed as he tossed another one onto the field. "Between all the teeth and claws, it doesn't take very long until one gets popped."

"We can replace that one." Ty snickered. "Since it was Avery who destroyed it."

I glanced over and saw the looks of love my mates had focused on me. Running toward them as everyone went to line up for another kickoff, I turned my claws inward and put my front paws on Ty's shoulders. I gave his face a big lick as he laughed and pushed me back down. While he was still laughing, I had an idea. His groin was right in front of my face, so I stuck my muzzle into it.

"Cut that out, Avery." Ty gasped. "I find your half and half form hot, but straight saber form is way too close to bestiality for me, baby."

"Stick in the mud." Cord snorted as he squatted down and petted me. He leaned in and whispered so no one else could hear us, "You can lick me with that big tiger tongue anytime you want to, baby."

I purred loudly as he scratched behind my ears. When I heard snarls and roars coming from my team, I realized I was holding up the game. I gave Cord's face a quick lick before racing off to my side of the field. After the next snap, I noticed lots of people had pulled over chairs and coolers as they watched the game.

The wolves weren't as good at football as my family. When we hit half time, we all shifted back and pulled on our shorts before going for refreshments. I walked right up to Cord, who was sitting in a chair talking with my mom and Alpha Daniels, and sprawled myself over his lap.

"I'm parched," I panted, smiling up at him.

"Well, we can't have that, baby." He chuckled, leaning forward to give me a quick kiss. He moved me off his lap, stood, and went to get me something to drink as I took his seat.

"I was just telling your mother and Cord how much fun my pack is having," Alpha Daniels said, taking a swig of his beer. "It was wonderful that you included all of us."

"You helped me find my family," I answered, catching my mom's gaze. "Your pack will always be welcome to any outing we have."

"And our family owes you a debt of gratitude," my mother continued. "I can never thank you enough, Alpha Daniels."

"I was glad to help," the Alpha replied with a smile. "I knew when my sweet girl was taken that she'd ended up being murdered. When Martin contacted me the first time, I knew the pain your family was going through. On top of that, to not know what happened to Avery was an extra injury I wouldn't wish on my worst enemy."

"Sorry about your daughter," I said gently, patting the Alpha's hand.

"Thank you, Avery." He smiled sadly at me. I was glad Cord walked up then with a bottle of water for me. I didn't know what else to say to Alpha Daniels. Cord leaned over to give me a quick kiss as he handed me the water.

"You really are one fast little guy, Avery." Cord chuckled as I downed as much water as I could without dumping it on myself.

"But I have endurance, too." I winked at him as I got up. Cord just shook his head as I sauntered back over to the game.

The rest of the party went off without a hitch. Everyone seemed to have a great time. At the end, everyone helped clean up. When I realized Trey was nowhere to be found, I asked my mom if she had seen him.

"I think your brother found one of his mates in the local pack." She snickered as she washed dishes.

"Oh, my, being mated to a werewolf should be interesting." I giggled.

It ended up the rest of my family decided to make the drive back to their house, saying two hours wasn't that big of a deal. Also, no one had packed anything for overnight, just jumped in the car as soon as they heard I was okay.

"I'm glad we did this," Cord said as we were waving goodbye to my family as they pulled out of the driveway. "But I might sleep for the next couple of days. I think we should call the kid next door to do the chores tomorrow."

"Yeah, I like that he's saving up for college," Ty agreed as we headed back inside.

"Too bad you guys are so tired. I thought we could have some fun in the pool alone," I purred.

"I vote for the hot tub. It's starting to get too cool at night for the pool," Cord replied as he locked up the front door.

"You have a hot tub? How big *is* this house?" I laughed.

"It's not in the house," Ty answered as he swooped me up into his arms. "You haven't seen the barn yet."

"A hot tub in a barn?" I asked, thinking they were pulling my leg.

"It was easier to put an outdoor hot tub in the barn so we could use it year round than convert a room in the house to have an indoor one." Cord shrugged as we walked out the backdoor onto the deck. Ty was so focused on getting my clothes off he almost tripped on the stone walkway as we headed to the barn.

"Walk first, strip after." I giggled, afraid he was going to drop me.

"I can do both," Ty replied defensively. Trying to make him feel better, I licked the side of his neck. He started walking much faster, almost running after Cord opened the barn door. I gasped when I saw the huge eight-person hot tub in the back corner of the barn. Ty set me on my feet and went to turn it on as I helped Cord out of his clothes.

"Are you guys done playing hard to get?" I purred as I unzipped his fly.

"Yes, I remembered to grab the waterproof lube," Cord answered before kissing me. I heard the jets kick on as we broke apart. "You have to give it a few minutes to warm up."

"What could we do until then?" Ty asked as I felt his naked body against my back. "I think we said you were going to beg us with our dicks in your mouth."

"My pleasure." I hissed as I dropped to my knees in front of them. I moved so I had each of their hard cocks in my hand. They got the idea and stood shoulder to shoulder, angling so there was just enough room in between them for me. Bringing both dicks to my mouth, I licked the slits in their cocks at the same time.

"We're still going to spank you later, baby." Cord moaned as he grabbed the back of my head. I merely grunted as I sucked on the heads of their cocks. Having both of them in my mouth made me wonder what it would feel like to have both dicks in my ass in the same time. Maybe something to try another time.

I could only take both of them about a quarter of the way in my mouth before I felt as if my lips would split open. Wanting more, but not willing to rush this, I licked, sucked, and even nibbled every inch of my mates' dicks.

"Fuck this, I'm going to blow soon." Ty growled as he pulled out of my mouth and lifted me up and over his shoulder. His hand landed hard on my ass. "I want to shoot my load in this sweet ass."

"Oh, god, do that again." I moaned, squirming on his shoulder. The pressure it put on my cock was just on the side of painful, and I loved it.

"Like this, baby?" he asked as he slapped my cheeks a few more times.

"Yes," I hissed. He put me down on the side of the hot tub. I let out a yelp, my ass now sensitive. Cord and Ty climbed into the hot tub and immediately reached for me. They spun me around so I was kneeling on one of the seats, my hands braced on the side of the tub. Sitting on either side of me, Cord smacked my ass a few times.

"I don't like that other shifters got to see my naked mate today," he said firmly. "Only we should get to see you naked."

"It was only right before and after I shifted," I argued.

"Don't talk back during your punishment," Ty grumbled as he spanked me hard a few times. "Or we'll just spank you and fuck each other, leaving you to watch."

"Who does this ass belong to, Avery?" Cord asked, smacking my ass on each word.

"You and Ty only," I moaned, leaning over more so they had more access to me.

"Oh, look at that pretty pink hole, Cord." Ty purred. He rubbed his fingers over it slowly, just to tease me. I let out a whimper, but didn't say anything. Then, suddenly, one of them spanked my asshole. I gasped in shock before letting out a carnal growl.

"I think he likes that, Ty." Cord chuckled. "Did you want us to do that again, baby?"

"Please, yes, anything." I moaned. "Spank me, finger me, rim me, fuck me. I don't care. I'm yours to do with whatever you want."

"Good answer, Avery," Ty replied. I felt two lubed fingers get shoved into my ass. Crying out in pleasure from the penetration, I squirmed around at the burning sensation.

"Fuck me, please, shove that big cock in my ass," I whimpered.

"We need to stretch you out more, sweetheart," Cord said as he ran his hand over my ass. "I like the way my handprint looks on his firm little ass."

"I like the burn. Please fuck me." I moaned, his words snapping my control. I pushed back hard on Ty's fingers, trying to get him to rub over my sweet spot.

"You're going to ride my cock while Cord fucks your face, Avery." Ty purred. Then, he bit the cheek of my ass hard.

"Yes, anything you want," I cried out. Ty pulled his two fingers from my ass and spun me around. Instantly, he started to lower me onto his cock. I wasn't stretched out as much as normal, so he had to really work to get inside of me. The pleasure-pain sensations were almost enough to have me come right then. Cord stood up in front of me then and held his dick up to my face. Before he even said anything, I took it into my mouth greedily.

"He's so goddamn tight." Ty hissed as he finally bottomed out inside of me. I moved my legs on either side of his thighs and when he spread them, he went in even deeper in me. I was overwhelmed with sensations—Ty inside me, the warm water splashing all around us as I sucked off Cord. Groaning around the cock down my throat, Cord grabbed the sides of my head and started to pump himself in and out of me.

"I need more." Cord moaned. "Ty, sit on the side of the tub, so I can fuck you while Avery rides you."

"Oh, hell yeah," Ty cried out as he slammed me down on his cock. Holding me in place, he moved us up onto the lip of the tub. "I figured you might want my ass."

"What does that mean?" Cord chuckled as he reached down to stroke my dick as he fingered Ty's hole.

"I stretched myself out when everyone was starting to leave." Ty moaned, his cock twitching inside me. I leaned back against his chest, wiggling on his lap, reveling in the feeling of Cord's touch and filling so full from Ty's dick.

"That's fucking hot, Ty," Cord groaned as he pulled his fingers out and started pushing his dick into Ty. We all moaned as Cord started to thrust in and out of Ty. Every time Cord started to pull out, Ty lifted me off his cock. And when he pushed back in, Ty slammed my hips back down. It was like my own personal roller coaster of heaven. Cord reached out and pinched one of my nipples hard. That was all it took to push me over the edge.

I cried out as I shot stream after stream of my seed all over Cord's hand and our stomachs. Ty sunk his teeth into my right shoulder as Cord leaned forward and did the same on my left. I had one of the most intense orgasms of my life, more cum erupting from my cock then I thought could fit in my balls. And it just kept going. The harder Cord fucked Ty and he fucked me, it was like a high I couldn't come back down from.

"I'm coming," Ty screamed as his cock exploded inside of me. When he was done, the two of us slumped down against each other as Cord continued to pound into Ty.

"No passing out. I'm not nearly done." Cord growled as he lifted me off Ty's lap. Flipping me over, Cord stood me in front of him and bent me in half so my face ended up in Ty's groin. "Lick him clean, baby. I'm going to fuck this sweet ass nice and hard."

"Yes," I purred as I started to lick Ty's half-hard cock. Cord slammed his cock into me fully in one thrust. I screamed in pleasure. The water kept splashing up against my dick, stomach, and chest, completely in contrast to the cooler air on my back.

"So good, baby. So fucking good." Cord grunted as he pounded into me and kept smacking my ass. "I know how we're going to mark you, Avery, as you did us."

"I bet I'm thinking the same thing you are, Cord," Ty moaned as I kept slowly licking his cock. "You want to pierce his hot little nipples."

"Oh, yeah," Cord answered. He leaned forward and pinched my nipples. I immediately cried out and started to go to town on Ty's cock. "See? It's a major hot spot for our baby."

"Harder." I hissed, loving all the sensations going through my body. Cord obliged me, and I swallowed all of Ty's cock. It hardened in my mouth as I sucked on it fiercely. I was incredibly blessed with men who could recover quickly. Just thinking about them wanting me this much got me hard all over again, as well.

"Fuck, fuck, fuck, baby," Cord chanted as he thrust as hard as he could into me. He screamed as he came inside me. The force of it was so hard I felt as if someone stuck a geyser in my ass. Finally, when he was done, he pulled out of me and plopped down on one of the seats in the hot tub. I pulled my mouth off Ty's cock and stared at it.

"I want more." I growled, moving to straddle him again. I grabbed his dick and held it against my hole as I slid back down on it. Staring into Ty's eyes, I saw them almost roll into the back of his head. "Bite my nipples while I ride you."

"Anything my mate wants." Ty moaned as I lifted myself back off before plunging right back down. His hot mouth clamped on my left nipple, and I went wild. I rode him as if he was a bucking bronco, bracing my hands on his shoulders. Ty smiled up at me as he pinched my right nipple while he bit down hard on my left one. He reached around and grabbed the cheeks of my ass as he helped me ride him. They were still incredibly sensitive from the spanking, and the pressure he put on them as I fucked myself on his cock was amazing.

"Yes, god. Yes, Ty. I need more," I screamed loudly. I wasn't even sure if the sex had been this animalistic during my honeymoon heat, but I loved every dirty second of it. Ty switched nipples then, biting down on my right nipple hard enough to leave teeth marks. My climax hit me fast. As the first stream of my cum hit Ty's stomach, I felt the muscles in my ass clamp down on his cock.

"Yeah, that's it, baby. Ride that cock." Cord groaned from behind me. "So fucking hot."

"You're not going to be able to walk for a week," Ty grunted as he lifted his head up from my chest. He had to have been close to his orgasm, as well, because he started thrusting up into me as hard as I slammed down. I was still coming as he shot his load inside of me. I cried out at the overwhelming sensations, clinging onto Ty as if my life depended on it.

When we were both finally spent, I slumped forward against him, his cock still in my ass. "That was fucking awesome." I panted. I gently licked my mating mark on Ty as we both tried to get our breathing back under control.

"It was just as amazing to watch." Cord chuckled. It took the rest of the energy I had left to look over my shoulder at him. But it was totally worth it. I giggled as I stared at his now spent cock in his hand. He had been jacking off as he watched me and Ty fuck like rabbits.

"Next time, we should bring a camera." I giggled then groaned when Ty lifted me off of him. I was like a wet noodle as I slid down into the hot tub onto one of the seats. The hot water and jets felt wonderful against my overworked muscles. My ass was still pretty tender, so that was a little uncomfortable.

"We were serious about getting those nipples pierced, baby," Cord said hesitantly as he swam over to me. "I was thinking about it earlier today. I want to get special rings made up, engraved like wedding rings. I know it's not legal for us to get married in this state or for all three of us to marry anywhere. But I thought since we have your mating marks, I want to mark you as ours, as well."

"I love the idea as much as I love you both," I whispered, pulling him down to my mouth. The kiss was gentle since I was wiped. He lifted me up against him, turned us around so we switched places, and sat back down. I could tell he was happy that I'd said yes. His kisses were sweet and filled with love.

"Hey, where's my sugar?" Ty chuckled. He sat down next to us, and Cord lifted me off his lap and handed me over to Ty. I felt bad I was like spent deadweight, unable to move myself. But they seemed to revel in the fact that they'd fucked me silly. Ty's soft lips came down on mine the moment I was in his arms. I threw my limp arms over his shoulders and melted into the kiss. When we broke apart, I rested my head on his shoulder. The instant my head stopped moving, I was out like a light.

Chapter 7

I was back on stage at the slimy circus that held me, wearing the collar that sent enough electricity in me to jump-start a car if I tried to escape. And they were whipping me, ordering me to perform. Everywhere I looked, people were yelling and throwing shit at me. I tried to get off stage, but they shocked me, and I collapsed.

Waking from my nightmare, I pushed Cord and Ty off me and ran to the bathroom. I made it just in time to throw up in the toilet. Once my stomach was empty, I crawled into the shower and turned the cold on full blast. Ty burst into the bathroom after me.

"Cord, get in here!" he yelled, racing into the shower with me. Ty sat on the cold tile and pulled me onto his lap. "It's okay, baby. I've got you now. No one can hurt you anymore."

"I'm sorry," I chattered out, holding onto him tightly. Cord was suddenly there behind me, hugging me, as well. He reached up and shut off the water, but we were already soaked.

"Did you have a nightmare, Avery?" Cord asked gently, rubbing my back. I nodded against Ty's shoulder, unable to talk for the moment. "You can talk to us, baby."

"I know," I whispered, trying to control my emotions enough to talk about it. "I was back at the circus on stage."

"You don't have to explain, Avery. We just want you to know we're here for you if you want to talk," Ty replied, interrupting me.

"I don't want to talk about it then, if that's okay?" I sniffled. I really didn't want to start crying against my mate. I already felt like such a wimp.

"I'm going to go start breakfast," Cord said, giving me a quick kiss on the top of my head.

"Don't leave me," I begged, reaching out to him. I stared up at him, knowing my eyes were filled with tears. He nodded and knelt back down.

"Can we move this to the bed, Avery?" Ty asked, standing when I nodded. He carried me to the bed, laying me down gently. Cord climbed into bed, as well, spooning my back as I lay against Ty's side.

"Will you make love to me? I need to feel my mates," I whimpered. I knew I sounded needy and scared, but I had to trust that they wouldn't judge me.

"Do you think that's the best idea after a nightmare like that?" Cord asked carefully.

"Yes, I want to replace all the bad memories with good," I answered, looking over my shoulder at him. I tried to beg him with my eyes, and it must have worked because he leaned forward and nipped my lower lip.

And make love we did. It was slow, passionate, loving, and tender sex like I'd never had before. I lay on my back as Ty took me while Cord was inside Ty. I wrapped my arms around Ty's neck and my legs around both of them. It was perfect. Magical, even. I could see both of their handsome faces and loving glances they gave me at the same time.

"Never leave me," I begged when we were done. "I couldn't ever survive it if you guys ever left me or didn't want me anymore."

"I want you and love you more every day, Avery," Ty said gently. Cord nodded, too choked up to speak right then. We all separated and, without a word, went back to the bathroom to shower together. Of course, calling it a shower was almost like calling a waterfall a sprinkler. The shower was massive enough for at least five adults to stand in. Granted, they wouldn't have much room to shower with that many people, but it was perfect for three.

There were four different shower heads and an overhead sprinkler that simulated rainfall. You turned on each separately, in case it was just one person showering or all of us, like right now. We washed each other, needing to touch as much of one another as we could. Sharing several heated, three-way kisses made us all get hard again, but this wasn't about sex. It was about remembering we were all there for each other and tied together.

"How about a special treat for breakfast today?" Cord asked when we were done and drying off. "I think we should get out the Belgian waffle maker. Don't you, Ty?"

"You are the greatest man anyone could ever ask for," Ty moaned and kissed him. "I love your waffles almost as much as I like that huge cock of yours in my ass."

"We're so hitting the adult store after we get Avery's nipples pierced." Cord chuckled as he cupped Ty's groin. "I think we should get one of every toy and try it out to see what we like."

"You don't know what you like?" I asked as I put my used towel in the hamper.

"We'd never been with a man until we met you, baby." Ty shrugged. "And we love that. Imagine what else there is out there we might like."

I felt cold as I clutched my chest, feeling like my heart just shattered. I pushed past both of them and stormed out into the bedroom. Taking several deep breaths before I turned to face them, I tried to get my anger under control.

"I will not fucking share either of you." I snarled. "I'm sorry that you weren't with other men before we all mated, but that doesn't give you the right to fuck around."

"Avery," Ty started to say, but I kept talking right over him.

"These are mine," I yelled, grabbing both their cocks. "I will not share them with anyone outside of this room. And, so help me, if anyone else ever touches them, I will rip them to shreds."

"Avery, listen to us," Cord said, placing his hand over my mouth. I tried to pull away, but Ty wrapped his arms around me to keep me still. "We don't want anyone else, baby. We were talking about other *things* to try, as in toys. Maybe some butt plugs, flavored lube, or some handcuffs. Not playing with *someone* else."

"Oh," I whispered, completely embarrassed when he removed his hand. "I thought you were saying I wasn't enough for you."

"Are you kidding? You're an animal in bed." Cord snickered, winking at me. "I just thought it might be fun to try some other things in bed. I mean, look how much you loved being spanked."

"Sorry," I replied, hugging him and Ty to me. "I'm really possessive and jealous."

"You think?" Ty chuckled. "Don't worry, baby. We are, too."

"I should never have doubted your loyalty to me," I said, staring up at them. "How can I make it up to you both?"

"Hmm." Cord purred as he reached down and squeezed my ass. "I think we might have to spank our bad, bad mate later. How about if we each get to pick out a toy that you promise to try out for us?"

"As long as it's not any whips or chains," I answered quietly, glancing quickly at the floor. "I don't think I could ever be tied down or whipped."

"The idea of whips is a turn off," Ty said gently as he lifted my head up. "Handcuffs kind of turn me on, but after what you've been through, we understand why you're not okay with them. I think we should handcuff Cord down one night. Make Mr. Dom here submit to us."

"I'd be willing to try that," Cord answered, clearing his throat. He seemed to really like the idea as his hard cock poked my stomach suddenly. "Are we okay now, Avery?"

"We're perfect." I smiled at them. "Now feed your hungry mate."

"With food or cock?" Ty chuckled, throwing my words from the first day I was with them back at me.

"Both. Always both." I giggled. They both looked at me with lust, but before they could do anything about it, I turned and raced downstairs to the kitchen. When I got there, I sat down at the table and folded my hands in my lap, pretending to be oh-so-innocent. Seconds later, Cord and Ty ran into the room and burst out laughing.

"Oh, yeah, nothing dirty just came out of your mouth." Cord snickered as he started pulling items out of the cabinets.

"I don't know what you mean," I replied sweetly, batting my eyelashes at them. "I simply wanted a front-row seat to watch you cook naked."

"And give me ideas of what to do to your naked body with the cooking oil," he mumbled so Ty and I could hear. We had another round of laughs before the waffles got underway. Cord cooked while we all chatted about the day ahead and what we wanted to do.

The waffles were amazing. Cord even topped them with some whip cream that he "accidentally" squirted on both me and Ty, which he then proceeded to lick off of us. Mine was along my collar bone, and his tongue made me turn into goo. Somehow, we made it through breakfast, got everything cleaned up, dressed, and into the car without jumping each other.

"So, you're really okay with this, Avery?" Ty asked as we pulled up to a jewelry store in Billings.

"Sure," I answered, hopping out of the truck. When they both stood there looking at me with a raised brow, I tried again. "It's not like I've always wanted to get my nipples pierced, but I'm not against it, either. And my mates are hot for the idea, so I'm more than willing to try it and see if I like it. I mean, you guys won't get mad if I hate it, will you?"

"No, not at all." Cord chuckled as he hugged me. "We just don't want you to do it only because we want it."

"I'm honored you came up with a way to mark me as yours," I answered, standing on my tiptoes to give him a kiss. I did the same with Ty, and then walked toward the store's door. I heard them laughing behind me. Not really sure what I did that was funny, but I knew they weren't laughing at me, so I was just glad they were happy. They followed me into the store, and I let them take over.

"May I help you gentlemen?" the salesman asked.

"Yes, we're looking for some smaller, platinum earrings that can be engraved," Cord answered, taking charge as always.

"I have just the thing," the man answered, opening up a display case. "Any woman would love to have these."

"Actually they're for our man, Avery." Ty snickered. "And they're going in his nipples."

"That's a new one for me." The man chuckled, smiling widely. "To each his or her own."

"Glad you see it that way," Cord answered. We all looked over the earrings the man held in a box. "What do you think, baby?"

"I like if they're not too expensive," I replied, feeling bad I never paid for anything.

"This is much cheaper than buying wedding rings, Avery," Ty said gently. "Just get whatever you like."

"These are small enough that I don't think I'll constantly be catching them on shirts." I nodded. "I think they're perfect."

"Excellent," the salesman answered. "What would you like engraved on them?"

"We want one to say 'Cord's' and the other to say 'Tyson's,'" Cord told him.

"Please write it out exactly how you want it and give me half an hour," the man said. Cord did as he asked, and a few minutes later, we were back in the truck heading to the adult store. As we pulled into the parking lot, I almost bounced right out of the truck. I was so excited to go to my first dirty store.

"Just wait until we get you home and use everything on you." Ty hissed in my ear as he hugged me from behind. I felt the evidence of how much he liked the idea pressing against my lower back. Still giggling, we walked through the open door Cord was holding for us.

When I stepped inside, I froze, wanting to turn around and run. "Avery, are you okay?"

"Holy shit," I gasped. "I don't know whether to be turned on or frightened."

"I'd prefer turned on, but if you're not comfortable here, we can leave," Cord said, taking my hand.

"I couldn't do this alone," I answered, snuggling against his side. "But my big, strong men are here. It's okay, I want to see what they have. I'm just a little overwhelmed."

"I was, too, my first time here." Ty laughed as he led the way. "I walked in and walked right back out three times. The fourth time, I finally took more than two steps in. I grabbed the first dirty magazine, paid for it, and ran."

"Some of those dildos would tear me in two," I whispered as we walked past the display on the wall. "But the idea of you guys using one on me totally turns me on."

"Let's start small. Maybe a couple of butt plugs and cock rings," Cord answered. "We can always come back and work our way up to dildos."

"Okay." I giggled, running my hand over his ass. I saw by the bulge in his jeans that it affected him. We stopped in the aisle of men's toys, and I let go of his hand so I could look at everything. I picked out a cock ring that vibrated with a gel extension that was supposed to rub right over your prostate. Holding it up to Ty, he winked at me and tossed it in the basket he was carrying. Cord moved down the aisle a bit, looking over several items before choosing a few and bringing them back to Ty.

"We definitely need some more lube and some waterproof stuff since Avery likes the pool and hot tub." Cord purred. I instantly got hard at the mention of the hot tub. "Oh, and one of these."

He tossed it in the basket before I could see what it was, and then met my gaze and wiggled his eyebrows at me. I could only imagine what he was picking out for me. We kept looking at items, laughing the whole time, before we finally filled up the basket. After heading to the register, the girl rang us up discreetly and bagged everything. Cord paid, and we left, got in the truck, and headed back to the jewelry store.

Once there, Cord ran inside and got the earrings. Back in the truck, he drove us to a tattoo parlor. Again, when we went inside, I felt a little apprehensive. There were a few very large, completely tattooed guys that screamed someone you didn't want to meet in a dark alley. Cord told the guy at the counter what we wanted. After paying, the guy led me over to a dentist's chair and told me to take off my shirt.

Another guy came over a few minutes later, holding a very scary stapler-type thing. He smiled and told me to relax then wiped my left nipple with an alcohol swab. It was cold, and my nipple instantly hardened. He took it between his meaty fingers, pushed the long needle against my skin, and stuck it in. I yelped in pain, not ready for how much it hurt. Realizing I'd worried Cord and Ty, I smiled widely at them. The guy did the same thing with my other nipple, and that was it. I was done.

I got up and went over to one of the floor-length mirrors to check it out. Touching the rings gently, I saw the engravings and started to tear up. It was the most wonderful, loving thing anyone had ever done for me. Meeting my men's gazes in the mirror, I saw they were as happy as I felt. I turned and hugged them both, groaning when my newly pierced nipples rubbed against their shirts.

"We're going to have to be very gentle with these babies for a while." I chuckled as Cord handed me my shirt. "Just the feeling of your shirts had me almost coming in my pants."

"Oh, don't tell us that until we're home, baby." Ty hissed in my ear as we left the store. "We're liable to fuck you on the ride home."

"I'm okay with that." I snickered as we climbed into the truck. Cord didn't say a word as we pulled out of the parking lot, and I started to worry I said something wrong. He drove about five minutes out of the city, and then veered off to the side of the road and put the truck in park. Before I could ask what was going on, he unlatched his seatbelt and mashed his lips down on mine. I wrapped my arms around his neck as he undid my belt, as well, and pulled me onto his lap.

"I love you so much, Avery," Cord whispered against my lips before delving back in my mouth. "You are the hottest little thing I've ever seen. You and Ty are the most perfect men ever."

"I love you, too," I replied, staring into his eyes. "Are you all right, Cord?"

"Yes, better than all right." He smiled at me. "I'm just so fucking happy. Sometimes, I think I'm going to burst from it."

"We feel the same way," Ty said gently, realizing, as I did, that it was hard for Cord to put his feelings into words. "But I'm also horny as hell."

"I got a special toy for our baby." Cord chuckled as he undid my fly. "I want to put it in you right now, Avery."

"Okay," I panted as he pulled my jeans down to my ankles. He moved me to straddle his lap as Ty dug through the bags. He opened a bottle of lube and squirted some on Cord's fingers. Cord pulled me toward him so my ass was spread open for him. He rubbed two fingers over my hole before sliding one in. "Fuck, that feels good."

"It looks even better from where I am." Ty groaned, rubbing his hand over his groin. Cord quickly stretched me out, sliding in two, then three fingers. I saw Ty open a small package and hand part of it to Cord. I wondered what was left in the bag. Cord pulled his fingers out of my ass, spreading the leftover lube on what I guess was some type of butt plug. Then, he slowly worked it inside of my ass. I cried out when it was finally all the way in me.

"What now?" I gasped as he wiggled the end of it around in my ass.

"Now, we put in the batteries." Ty snickered as he pulled the other part out of the bag. I glanced over and saw it was a tiny remote control.

"What does it do?" I asked as Cord pulled back up my jeans and moved me back to my seat. Even simply sitting down with it in my ass had me groaning and squirming. I was started to desperately need to come.

"It expands and vibrates while in your ass," Cord answered as he licked my ear. "We're going to drive you insane with need as we drive home. You're going to be so ready for us to fuck you, you won't know what to do with yourself."

"Dirty, dirty mate," I purred, leaning over and deliberately licking my mating mark on them. He shivered, feeling the need to join when I did that. Cord shook his head and chuckled as he threw the truck back into drive. I was just about to reach over and rub my hand over his groin when Ty did something with the toy. Gasping, I moved in my seat as the plug in my ass got bigger. "Fuck, I'm so going to blow in my pants."

"Take off your shirt now, Avery." Cord growled, his knuckles turning white on the steering wheel. I did as he asked, slowly pulling it off so I didn't irritate my sensitive nipples. He reached over and flicked my left ring, the one with his name on it. I moaned loudly and started rubbing my ass against the seat. "So beautiful. Absolutely, fucking hot."

"I love you, too." I hissed out as Ty pushed another button. The plug got bigger again and started to vibrate slightly in my ass. "Please, I need to play with my cock."

"No," they both answered me, but then Ty continued. "No touching yourself. We want you insane with lust."

"I'm always insane with lust for my hot mates," I whimpered as Ty leaned over and licked his ring. "Oh, fuck, this is going to kill me."

"Come for us, baby," Cord ordered as he kept playing with his ring. I reached back and grabbed the top of my seat with both hands so I didn't touch myself. They were right. I was losing my mind with need. Ty kept licking and sucking on one ring, and Cord was playing with the other as the thing in my ass started to vibrate more. "Ty, unzip him. I want to see when he comes."

"Fuck, fuck, fuck," I chanted softly as Ty undid my jeans and pulled out my throbbing cock. He quickly let it go and went back to sucking my nipple. Ty must have pushed another button because the plug got bigger again, and that was all it took. I screamed as I climaxed, shooting my cum all over myself and the truck's dashboard. Humping my hips in the air moved the plug in my ass in time to the wave of my orgasm. Light burst behind my eyes as I just kept coming, wave after wave.

"Yeah, baby, ride it out." Cord groaned as he pulled on his ring. It shot more sensations throughout me as I started coming all over again.

"I can't. No more. It's too much," I cried out as Ty sucked on my nipple harder. The plug in my ass went nuts to the point I could feel the vibrations throughout my stomach.

"We got you, sweetheart," Cord cooed as my cock just kept shooting more and more cum everywhere. "We'll catch you. Just enjoy it."

I mumbled something completely incoherent as more lights burst behind my eyes, and then everything started to go black. I heard Cord say he loved me before the darkness pulled me under.

Chapter 8

"Frank, we've got four strange guys on our property looking around," I heard Cord say into the phone. "I'm thinking we've got problems."

My eyes flew open as I heard the safety click off a handgun. I sat up in time to see my men head to the front door, guns in hand. Quickly, I crawled to the front window and peered out from behind the curtain. My heart started to race as I recognized two of the men as hunters who held me prisoner.

"You're on our land," Cord called out from the front porch.

"Sorry about that," Zac Rollins said, turning on his charm. He was the main guy who ran the circus and captured all the shifters. "My name is Mr. Smith. We've been tracking a very dangerous wild animal that escaped our care. Have you boys seen any tigers around here recently?"

Mr. Smith? Yeah, and I'm Santa Claus.

"No, and I think you need to leave before we call the sheriff," Ty answered firmly.

"Funny, you've got several sets of tiger tracks on your land," Jack Mason replied. He was the real asshole, beating and raping every shifter he could get his hands on. "I'd say the tiger spent a good deal of time here before moving on if he's not still here."

"Are you calling me a liar?" Cord asked. His tone of voice sent shivers down my spine. I'd never heard him use that tone before. "You need to get the fuck off my property. I won't tell you again before we start shooting."

"We're federal agents, Mr. Hartwell. I wouldn't do that," Zac replied with a smirk. "We've heard you have a new man in your life, a smaller guy with orange hair."

"Are you looking for some escaped tiger or a man?" Ty asked, raising an eyebrow. "And if you're feds, I want to see badges."

"Absolutely," Jack answered, reaching into his jacket. I saw the flash of metal, and knew it was a gun. Taking two quick steps back, I leaped with everything I had, shifting on the fly as I broke through the front window. I knocked Ty out of the way as Jack pulled the trigger, hitting me squarely on the right side of my chest. It hurt like a motherfucker, and I knew I was in bad shape. But I didn't care. My mates were still in danger. Moving faster than the humans could, I jumped up and sunk my teeth into one guy's neck then tossed him aside like a limp doll.

I heard a few more gunshots but ignored them as I continued to take out the threat. Leaping at Zac, I was able to tear out his throat, but he shot me in the side at point blank range. I heard sirens in the distance and prayed that they got here soon. Cord or Ty had shot the other stranger dead and put numerous holes into Jack.

"Avery!" Ty screamed as he fell to his knees in front of me. I shifted back as I heard the skidding of tires breaking too fast. Collapsing in his lap, I saw I had several holes in me as well. "Fuck, Cord, he's bad. What were you thinking, Avery?"

"Saw gun," I gasped out. "Couldn't let him shoot you."

"You're going to die, you piece of shit," Jack spat out. How the fuck was he still alive?

"Avery, oh god, Avery," Trey cried out as he knelt beside me.

"How are you here?" I asked, completely confused.

"I'll explain everything later, little bro. Just hang on," he answered. Cord came back with a large first-aid kit. Everyone got to work on me as Frank held a gun to Jack. They seemed to be arguing.

"How could you do this to your own people?" Frank growled, shaking with anger. "Our council will deal with you if you fucking live."

"Boo-fucking-hoo," Jack spat out. Frank holstered his gun and pulled Jack up on his feet, cuffing him. "Just because I was born a wolf doesn't mean shifters are my people."

"Wolf?" I gasped, completely shocked.

"He's hiding his scent somehow," Frank answered me. I held up my hand for him to hang on as I grabbed Trey's shirt and yanked him down to me.

"That's the one that raped me," I whispered in my brother's ear so no one else could hear. "Don't let him do it to anyone else."

"I promise, little brother," he answered, tears in his eyes. I could see the rage and questions he wanted to ask me in his eyes, but, like a good brother, he just stood and did what I asked. Trey gave Frank a nod, who raised an eyebrow at him. His hand shifted into claws as he stalked toward Jack. Trey moved his paw under Jack's groin and yanked upwards, definitely castrating the man. "Rape someone now you, son of a bitch."

Everyone stared at Trey with wide eyes as he spit in Jack's face. Frank didn't ask questions, just dragged a bleeding Jack to the police cruiser. Cord and Ty stared down at me, figuring out what I'd told Trey. I nodded to confirm their suspicions.

"Don't worry. His council won't let him live," Trey informed him as he knelt back by me. "I just gave him something to suffer through until then."

"Thanks, Trey." I hissed out as Cord extracted the bullet out of my side.

"Won't he heal from that?" Ty asked as he glanced up from working on my chest.

"The wound will heal and close, but his dick won't grow back." Trey snickered as he pulled off his belt. He wrapped it around my thigh and pulled it tightly. "He deserves worse, but we can't kill another shifter's kind without approval from their council. I mean, we can in a fight, but he was already caught."

"I would have released him again if I knew he was the one who raped Avery," Frank answered as he joined us again. "He can fucking bleed to death in the truck for all I care."

"Thanks, guys." I coughed, realizing it was getting hard to breathe. "He can't hurt me anymore."

"No, he can't, baby," Ty said as he pushed my hair away from my face. "Promise me you'll hang on, Avery. We can't lose you."

"Fuck, I ain't going anywhere." I gasped. "I want more Belgian waffles and sex from my mates now that they've marked me as theirs."

"I'll make you waffles for every goddamn meal if stay with us," Cord answered, tears running down his face. "I lost the only family I had before you and Ty. I won't lose anymore. You fucking stay with us, Avery."

"He's already healing, Cord," Trey said gently. "We need to get the last bullet out so he can shift and start healing."

"I got it," Ty exclaimed, removing it from my thigh. Trey undid his belt and gave me a nod before helping me roll on my side. I screamed as he did, shifting as soon as I was in position. The pain was immeasurable as I changed and then changed right back.

"I love you, mates," I whispered before blacking out.

* * * *

"It's my fault he's laying there like that," Cord shouted, and I realized it wasn't a dream. Opening my eyes, I saw Cord pacing around, waving his hands wildly. "He told us that he had hunters after him. Avery warned us that they'd never stop looking for him. Did I listen? No, I was making him waffles and fucking him on every surface known to man!"

"I enjoyed both immensely," I croaked out, my throat dryer than the desert. Ty and Cord raced to me immediately. I saw my mom and dads standing behind them, smiling widely.

"Don't ever do that again, baby." Cord growled at me.

"What, talk?" I asked, completely confused.

"No, put yourself in danger like that!" he answered, leaning over to kiss me. Ty pulled down the sheet to my waist, running his hands over my body.

"Everything's almost healed," Ty whispered. "We were so scared we lost you."

"I told you I would heal." I panted after Cord stopped kissing me.

"You didn't know that when you leaped out the fucking window," Cord said sternly. "Never again, Avery. Ty and I can take care of ourselves. You shouldn't have jumped in the way."

"So I was just supposed to let Ty get shot?" I asked, squinting my eyes at him. "You might be bigger than me, but I can take more damage than either of you. Would you stand by and do nothing as someone pulled a gun on me?"

"Of course not!" Cord yelled and stood up. "It's not the same, though."

"It's exactly—" I started to respond, but stopped short when I realized something was missing. My ring. The shot to my chest knocked off my right nipple ring—the one from Ty.

"Avery, what's wrong, sweetheart?" My mom asked, always the most observant one in the room.

"My ring." I sniffled, tears falling down my cheeks. "I lost Ty's ring."

"You were shot four times, almost died, and you're worried about some fucking ring? We can replace the goddamn ring," Cord screamed.

"Stop yelling at me," I cried, pissed at how he was treating me. "You said those rings were like wedding bands. People get upset when they lose their wedding rings."

"You didn't lose it." Cord leaned over and growled in my face. "It got blown off of you when you got fucking shot in the chest."

"I still don't have it anymore," I whispered as I started to move away from him. I didn't like this side of Cord, and I was almost scared to be near him. "You bought me those rings to mark me as yours. They're important to me."

He stared at me for several moments, gesturing in silence at my scooting across the bed. "Fine," he shouted, storming toward the bedroom door. "He's worried about a goddamn nipple ring instead of almost dying. It's just a fucking piece of metal."

I watched him leave the room, still yelling to himself as he went downstairs and out the front door. He slammed it so hard behind him that the frame of the house shook. I looked up at Ty at a complete loss for words.

"He's been through a lot while you've been out the past couple of days," my mom said gently, sitting on the bed by me. "Some people get angry when they're afraid."

I nodded, still not knowing what to say. After the silence became unbearable, I finally spoke. "Can I get something to drink?"

"Yes, then we're going to shower your stinky ass." Ty chuckled as he reached over to the night stand and grabbed me a glass of water. I drank it down greedily, thinking it was probably the best water I'd ever had. When I was done, I handed him back the empty glass.

"Fine, but I want to use the guest room," I answered, sitting up.

"Why don't you want to use our room?" Ty asked, raising an eyebrow at me.

"Because it doesn't feel like *our* room right now," I replied as he helped me stand. "Not with Cord acting like this and being so mad at me."

"He's not really mad at you. He thinks this is his fault," Beck said as everyone started to leave the room. I hobbled after them, every muscle, bone, and joint hurting in my body.

"Can I please carry you, Avery?" Ty hissed in my ear. "It's killing me to see you walk around in so much pain."

"Yes, please." I smiled up at him. He gently lifted me into his arms, and I snuggled against him. "This is what I wanted to wake up to."

"I know, baby," he answered, kissing me quickly. "Cord deals with grief and sadness differently than most do."

"What is there to be sad about? I'm fine," I said, still not getting it.

"We'll leave you to sort this all out." My mom chuckled as she came over and kissed me on the cheek. "We're staying in one of the spare rooms downstairs. I'm tired, so you get cleaned up, and we'll see you at dinner."

"Thanks for being here," I replied, feeling bad I was pretty much ignoring my parents. This thing with Cord just had me tied up in so many knots. My mom smiled at me as she patted my knee then turned and walked into both my dads' arms. They were always there, the strong, silent type. We turned and went down the hall to the other guest room with its own bathroom while they headed down the stairs.

"You scared the shit out of me, Avery," Ty said gently as he held me tighter. We made our way into the guestroom and then the bathroom. He sat me down on the counter as he went and turned on the shower. "I don't know what I'd ever do if I lost you."

"Don't you get it, Ty?" I sighed, starting to get annoyed with them. "I feel the same way. I couldn't just stand there and do nothing. The hunters were here because of me."

"I *do* get it, baby," he replied as he started to undress. "I'm not mad that you jumped in. I understand why you did it. I'm upset you got hurt, and I think I have a right to be upset about that."

"You're right. I'm sorry," I answered as I watched him pull his pants down. "I assumed you were mad like Cord. That was wrong of me."

"He's not mad at you. He's mad at himself," Ty said. He walked over to me in all his naked glory. I couldn't help myself from reaching down and stroking his cock. "He feels like he failed us by letting you get hurt."

"I don't understand that, but I don't want to talk about it anymore, either," I whispered, staring up at him. "Right now, I want to feel and love on my mate. I was scared, too, Ty. I saw the gun and thought I might lose you."

"I love you so much, Avery." He moaned. Ty leaned in to kiss me softly at first, but the faster I stroked him, the deeper the kiss went. "Baby, aren't you too hurt for this?"

"For sex, probably." I smirked up at him then stuck out my lower lip. "But I think we can play without me feeling any pain. I need to feel you right now, Ty."

"Me, too. You have no idea how much I need you right now, Avery," he replied. Ty pushed into my hand as he leaned down and licked my nipple ring. "We'll replace my ring. I know it meant a lot to you. It did to me, too. But it is replaceable. You aren't."

"Show me, Ty. Show me how much you need me." I hissed in his ear then licked over my mating mark on his shoulder. "I thought I was going to lose you."

"Thank you, Avery. You probably saved my life," Ty said firmly. He took my head in his hands and stared right in my eyes. "Thank you for loving me enough to risk yourself to save me."

"You would have done the same," I answered, tears forming in my eyes. "I need you inside me, Ty. We can go slow, and it won't hurt. But, god, I need to feel you."

"Me, too, my love," he whispered then mashed his mouth down on mine. I threw my arms over his shoulders and wrapped my legs over his hips. Ty dug in the pocket of his jeans he had tossed on the counter, pulling out a tube of lube. He lifted me off the counter as he squirted some slick on his hand.

"Will you let me rim you one day with my tiger tongue?" I asked, finally having the courage to verbalize what I'd been dying to know.

"You mean in your half and half form?" He answered as he moved us into the shower and closed the door behind us.

"Yes. You acted strange when we mated that way and I claimed you," I replied, searching his eyes. He got this pensive look on his face as we stepped under the water. I felt one of his fingers push into my ass, and I groaned softly.

"I told you I'm not into bestiality, and even your half and half form pushes it for me," Ty finally said. "I know that makes me a prick—"

I covered his lips with my hand, cutting him off. "You can't help how you feel, Ty. But it's not bestiality, even if I was in full tiger form. I'm not just an animal then, Ty. I'm still me, and I still know you're my mate. I love you just as much then as I do now in human form."

"I love you the same when you're in tiger form, baby," Ty whispered, his eyes never leaving mine. I whimpered when he slid a second finger into me and started scissoring them back and forth. "It's different sexually to me, though. I know we have to mate once a month with you in half and half, but that's about all I can handle. I hope you can understand that."

"Anything you want, Ty," I replied, realizing this wasn't easy for him. "I simply want us to be honest with each other, okay?"

"I promise," he said, smiling at me as he pushed in a third finger. I hissed as I held onto him tighter. "Am I hurting you?"

"No, feels fantastic," I replied as he leaned me against the wall. He pulled his fingers out of my ass and lowered me onto his hard cock. "I love you, Ty."

"As I love you, Avery. All of you," he answered after he bottomed out inside of me. I moved my hands to his shoulders as mine rested on the shower tile. It gave us a better angle for him to move inside me easier. "I love everything about you, sweetheart. I just can't fuck you or let you play with me when you're in tiger form."

"I don't want you when I'm full tiger." I panted as he took me slowly. It was incredibly intimate, staring at each other, moving together when we were completely focused on one another. "I want to figure out a way that you're more comfortable with me in half and half form."

"Give me time, baby." He grunted, and I knew he was holding back the need to pound my ass. "We've only been together a week and a half. This is all still new to me."

"That's what I needed to know," I replied, nodding. "I just needed to hear that you weren't disgusted that you had to have sex with someone who's part tiger."

"Avery, never!" Ty gasped, freezing his motions. "Is that what you thought this whole time?"

"I wasn't sure," I answered honestly. "I had to know the truth."

"Baby, I want you to listen to me carefully," Ty said, stroking my cheek. "I wouldn't be disgusted even if I fucked you in full tiger form. I'd be a little freaked and maybe somewhat uncomfortable, but never, ever disgusted. I know it's you under that fur, and I love you with all my heart."

"Thank you," I whispered, leaning forward to claim his lips. At least all my fears and doubts were settled with one mate. But right now, I couldn't think about everything with Cord. Instead, all I wanted was to make love to Ty. Moving my hips off of him, he got the idea and started thrusting in time with me again.

We gazed into each other's eyes, letting that look say everything and anything else that needed to be said. Some things simply cannot be put into words. Ty kept the pace slow and loving for several more minutes until we came together, crying out and holding onto one another.

When we were done, showered, and dried off, Ty moved us to the guest bed. Even though I'd been out for the past couple of days, I was still recovering and tired. I might be able to heal from almost anything, but even for a shifter, four bullet wounds was a lot to heal from. Lying there wrapped around Ty, I felt as if half my world was complete while the other half was in chaos. I didn't know what to do or what was going on with Cord.

Chapter 9

The next two days I spent mainly in bed recovering and healing. I'd spent lots of time with my parents and Ty, but Cord never came by. Finally, on the morning of the third day, Cord knocked on the door. Ty had gone downstairs to get us some breakfast, so we were alone. My parents had gone back to Wyoming knowing I was on the mend and the hunters were all dead.

"Baby, can I come in?" Cord asked hesitantly. I was lying on my side with my back to the door.

"It's your house. I can't stop you," I replied, not hiding my annoyance.

"Please? I found your ring," he begged. I rolled over and stared at him a few moments before speaking.

"Have you been looking for it this whole time?"

"Yes," he said quietly. It was then I noticed how red and puffy his eyes were from crying, but he wasn't looking at me. He held the ring up in his hand as he stared at the floor.

"Where did you find it?"

"Under the front porch," Cord replied, taking a few steps toward me. "It must have fallen in between the slats of wood. I kind of pulled up most of the porch to get it."

"Thank you, Cord. You didn't have to do that," I said gently, not sure what was going on. "I appreciate it."

"Does that mean you won't leave me?" he asked, finally glancing at me.

"Leave you? Who said anything about leaving?" I replied, completely shocked and confused.

"No one, but I acted like such a rat bastard I figured I lost you."

"Cord, come here, my mate," I said, holding my arms open to him. I heard his quick intake of air as his eyes searched mine. Seconds later, he was on the bed in my arms.

"I love you, Avery. I'm so sorry for being an asshole," he cried out, clutching me to him. "Can you ever forgive me?"

"There's nothing to forgive, Cord," I replied, running my hands over his back. "I'm just confused. You were so mad at me, and now you thought I was going to leave you because of one fight? Mating is forever, Cord. I love you, even when you're being a dumbass."

"Thank you, baby." He sobbed, his whole body shaking. "Please don't ever leave me. I'd die if you did."

"I'm not going anywhere," I said firmly as I took the ring from his hand. I set it on the nightstand, glad to have it. But, right now, my mate needed me. I just wasn't sure what was going on with him. "Cord, why were you mad at me? What's going on?"

"I thought I lost you," he cried as he peppered my neck with kisses. "You can't ever leave me, Avery. I wouldn't survive it. I love you so fucking much. I don't know how to deal with it."

"I love you, too, big guy," I said, trying to soothe him. "I'll never leave you."

"I love you, I love you," he chanted as he kissed and touched every inch of my body. Cord looped his fingers in my pajama bottoms and yanked them off of me. "I need you, Avery."

"You have me, Cord."

"No, I *need* you, baby," he whispered as he licked down my chest. "I thought I'd lost you. I need to feel every inch of you to make sure you're really here."

"I'm all yours, Cord." I groaned as he stopped and sucked on his nipple ring. I reached back over to the night stand and grabbed the bottle of slick. Handing it down to him, he snatched it out of my hand. I heard the cap snap and felt his lubed fingers rubbing my hole seconds later. I moaned loudly and squirmed under his touch.

"So fucking perfect." He hissed as he pushed a finger into my ass. "I'm so sorry, Avery. I'll never yell at you again. I'll do anything you want if you promise never to leave me."

"Cord, it's okay." I grunted as he pushed in a second finger. He was stretching me out as fast as he possibly could.

"No, it's not. I don't deserve you," he cried. I still wasn't sure what was going on with him besides Cord wanting inside me as soon as possible. Now didn't seem the time to get him to explain it to me, so I gave my mate what he needed.

"I'm ready, Cord." I panted as he slid in a third finger. "Take me, my mate."

"Are you sure you're stretched out enough?" he asked, his eyes begging me to say yes. I nodded at him and pulled off his shirt. Cord quickly removed his fingers from me, unzipped and yanked off his pants. He moved back to be bed seconds later, lubed up his cock, and started to push into me. "I've missed you, Avery."

"I was right here, Cord," I replied gently, taking his face in my hands. I didn't know what to say or how to help him with whatever demons were hounding him. We both moaned when he was finally seated all the way inside me. He looped his elbows under my knees and leaned down so that our faces almost touched.

"You're mine, Avery," he whispered against my lips as he started to thrust into me hard and fast. "Mine and Ty's. No one else can have you. Not God. Not anyone."

"All yours," I answered, not sure what to say.

"He's taken enough from me. He can't have you, too." Cord grunted, picking up the pace. He was pounding into me at a furious rate. Not knowing what else to do, I pulled his head down to mine and mashed our lips together. I'd never seen him this aggressive, and that's saying a lot because Cord was a pretty aggressive man. But it didn't seem to be aimed at me, just at the idea of losing me.

"I love you, Cord. I'll never leave you." I moaned as he lifted my hips up and started pegging my sweet spot. "No one but Ty can ever have me."

"I'll make waffles or pancakes or eggs or whatever you want every day, baby." He sniffled. Cord buried his head in my neck as he fucked me like an animal, so I couldn't see his face. "You can have whatever you want, Avery. We can buy a house closer to your family, or I can give you all the rings you want."

"I only want you, Cord," I replied, shocked at his outburst. "I don't need anything else but you."

"I'm not enough," Cord cried out, pounding into me even harder. It didn't hurt, but I'd never been fucked with quite so much strength. "You deserve better than me, and I don't know how to make up that difference so you'll stay. You can spank me if you want, baby. Tie me up and fuck me in tiger form, I don't care. I'll do whatever you want!"

I was just about to respond when he screamed out his orgasm and pumped his seed into me. Rubbing his arms and shoulders, I ran my fingers over my mating mark on him. "This mark means I will keep you forever, Cord," I said gently as he tried to catch his breath. "I love you just the way you are. You are more of a man than I could have ever dreamed one of my mates to be."

"I need more," he whispered as he pulled out of me, still rock hard. Cord gently flipped me over onto my stomach. He lay flush against my back as he pushed his cock inside of me again. Moving his arms under my shoulder, he clasped my hands as we leaned on our elbows. The angle was so different that I was even tighter for him this way. "I'm sorry. Once wasn't enough."

"Take me, my mate," I moaned as he started to pull back out. "Take everything I have to give, Cord."

"I need all of you, Avery," he said, choking on his sobs as he spoke. This time he took me slower and much gentler, and I loved it just as much as before. It was so intimate, being wrapped around each other like this, even if he couldn't see my face. He spread my legs apart wide with his, plunging into me so he hit my prostate every time. Though I was still confused and somewhat distracted, my body needed its release. Seconds later, I cried out as my climax hit me.

Cord taking my ass and the bedding rubbing against my cock was enough to push me over the edge. He must have felt it, turning us onto our sides so that my cock didn't spurt my seed all under me. Wave after wave of my orgasm hit me like a speeding bus to the point where I barely heard when Cord screamed out my name and came as well. We lay there panting for several minutes, trying to get our heart rates back under control.

"You need to tell him, Cord," Ty said softly from the doorway. I glanced up and saw tears in his eyes as I gave him a questioning look. "Avery won't understand what this is all about unless you tell him."

"He'll leave me if I do," Cord answered, burying his head in my shoulder. "I can't do it. I can't risk it."

"Cord, nothing you tell me will make me love you any less," I replied, starting to pull away from. I groaned as his spent cock slid from my ass. But Cord wasn't letting me go, so I had to forcefully pull away. I rolled over and held his head in my hands. "Cord, I'm not leaving you, no matter your past. But you told me you love me. Love means you're honest with each other."

Cord stared at me a few moments before finally nodding. He sat up and pulled me up to straddle his lap. Leaning his forehead against mine, he took several deep breaths. "I killed my parents."

"Cord!" Ty exclaimed, racing to the bed. "That's *not* what happened. It wasn't your fault. You were just a kid."

"It *was* my fault," Cord replied softly. "I forgot something in my class, so I went back to get it. I missed the bus, and the school's secretary called my parents to come get me. This guy driving a truck wasn't paying attention and hit them head on, killing everyone. They died instantly."

"Cord, it wasn't your fault. It was the other driver's," I said, glancing at Ty over Cord's shoulder. He knelt on the bed and crawled toward us before wrapping himself at Cord's back.

"It was my fault," Cord cried. "If I hadn't missed the bus, they never would have been in the car driving."

"All these years I never knew you thought it was your fault," Ty whispered, his eyes filling with tears. "No one ever blamed you, Cord. It wasn't your fault, sweets."

I placed my hand over Cord's mouth when he went to talk and interrupted him. "Was it my fault I got caught by hunters because I wasn't running right next to my parents?" I asked, waiting until he shook his head to continue. "Do you blame my parents for it?"

"No, of course not," he replied after he moved my hand off his lips. "I see your point, but it's not the same."

"Yes, it is," Ty said firmly. "We love you. Do you think either Avery or I would lie to you?"

"No," Cord whispered. "No, you wouldn't do that."

"Then you'll just have to believe us and know we can get through this, okay?" I said. He nodded as he pulled both of us down to the bed to lie on either side of him. Cord was out almost the moment his head hit the pillow. Ty and I stared at him and then at each other for a while. But what was there to really say? Instead, we nestled against our mate and took a nap.

* * * *

A few weeks later, it was the beginning of the lunar cycle. We had put the porch back together and installed a new, larger porch swing that fit the three of us comfortably. I had my nipple re-pierced with Ty's ring that Cord had found for me. Cord seemed to be doing much better mentally. I think finally sharing his guilt and grief about his parents lifted a weight from his shoulders none of us knew was there.

I was in the shower when I started to go into heat. Quickly finishing up, I shifted into half and half form. I grabbed the large bottle of lube and went in search of my mates. They were under the tractor working on something. What, I had no clue. I so wasn't the mechanical type. I watched them for several minutes, simply loving how they interacted and fought sometimes. The love I felt for them was amazing it completed my soul.

"Don't be an idiot, Ty. We can't just buy a new tractor every time something breaks down," Cord grumbled.

"Not *every* time," Ty replied, sounding unhappy, as well. "I'm just saying we don't have to be so tightfisted with money, Cord. This tractor is, like, twelve years old. Let the poor thing go."

"This was the first tractor we ever picked out and bought," Cord yelled. "And you want to just take it to the dump?"

"No, we should keep it," Ty shouted back. "I'm not saying get rid of it, simply retire the old girl, and get a new one for the daily stuff. I mean, how many times are we going to rebuild it?"

"You just don't like doing this part of ranching."

"You're damn right I don't! Hire someone else to do it if you won't get a new one," Ty exclaimed.

"Fine, go in the house then, you big baby." Cord snorted. "I can do this myself."

"Oh, no, you said it was a two-person job," Ty replied. "I'm not going to leave you so you can bitch that you had to do it all by yourself."

"I *am* doing it all by myself," Cord grumbled. "All you're doing is holding tools and bitching at me. *I wanna new tractor. I don't want to do this, Cord.*"

"I do *not* sound like that," Ty yelled. They were lying side by side, so I knelt one leg in between each of theirs and started to unzip their pants.

"Avery!" They both laughed.

"I'm in heat. I need to fuck and suck my mates." I growled. Careful of my claws, I reached in and pulled out their cocks. I stroked Ty's as I started licking Cord's. Both moaned loudly, and I heard whatever tools they were holding drop to the ground. It was kind of funny. I could only see the lower half of them, jeans open and dicks hanging out. "Besides, I got tired of listening to you two squabble."

"It's not night yet." Ty groaned as I worked up and down his cock with my hand.

"Doesn't matter. The lunar cycle starts before nightfall," I answered in between licks of Cord's huge dick. I'd known it was coming, so I'd already prepared myself before the shower and was nicely stretched out. But right now, I wanted inside my mates and to bite them, claiming them all over again. "Who am I fucking first?"

"Can we get out from under the tractor?" Cord asked, laughing his ass off.

"Fine," I grumbled, getting off of them. "But don't put those gorgeous cocks away. I'm feeling the need to take my mates outside."

"Whatever our baby wants." Ty snickered as they crawled out from where they were.

"Whatever I want?" I purred, rubbing myself all over him as he stood up.

"Within reason," Ty corrected. "What do you want, sweetheart?"

"I want to fuck Cord while eating your ass." I growled as I started shredding his clothes. Once he was standing there naked and laughing, I turned and did the same to Cord. "On your hands and knees, big man."

"Gladly," Cord replied, cupping my groin before he complied.

"Stretch him out, Ty." I hissed, loving the sight of my mate's ass presented to me like a gift. I knew I couldn't control myself or be gentle enough to stretch him out with my claws when I started going into heat.

"Can we shower first?" Ty asked, raising an eyebrow at me.

"No," I snarled as I yanked him down on to his knees. He moved so that he was facing Cord's ass and took the lube from me. They both chuckled at my impatience as Ty squirted some slick on his fingers. I got down on all fours and started licking the crack of Ty's ass. He gasped, and I remembered what he said about being uncomfortable with me doing that in any type of tiger form.

"Baby, why did you stop?" he asked, groaning and looking over his shoulder at me.

"I thought you didn't like me to do that with my tiger tongue?"

"I changed my mind." Ty chuckled as he pushed his ass in my face. "I love you. I know it's you, but it feels so fucking good I don't care if you're part or full tiger right now."

"Told you." Cord snickered as Ty scissored his fingers in Cord's ass. "Once you've been rimmed with Avery's huge, rough tongue, you're going to wander the house looking for him every time you want sex, going, 'here, kitty, kitty.'"

Ty and I froze, thinking about what Cord said before starting to laugh like loons. He rolled over and joined in as we all fell in a big pile on each other. This was what I'd always dreamed about when I thought of being mated. Mates I loved, couldn't get enough of, and just enjoyed spending time with.

THE END

WWW.JOYEEFLYNN.COM

Siren Publishing

Ménage Amour

My Little Kitty

JOYEE FLYNN

PURRFECT MATES 2

MY LITTLE KITTY

Purrfect Mates 2

JOYEE FLYNN
Copyright © 2011

Chapter 1

We had just finished beating the local werewolf pack at a game of football and I was parched. Jogging over to one of the many coolers, I reached in and pulled out a bottle of water. I saw my younger brother Avery sitting on the lap of one of his mates, Cord, and smiled. After all those years in captivity at that freak show circus, he deserved all the happiness finding his mates could give him.

Being the firstborn of our litter, technically I was the oldest and still felt guilt over his capture. I'd watched my parents suffer for almost thirty years as they grieved the loss of their youngest son. Though I had been just a boy myself, Avery was my baby brother and the need to protect him was ingrained in me.

Suddenly, I was snapped out of my thoughts of the past when I smelled the most delicious scent. *My mate*, I thought, glancing around. He realized his mate was here the second I found him. Still naked, I threw my water down and stalked over to him, my now hard cock slapping up against my stomach. I didn't even give him the chance to speak as I threw my arms around his neck and mashed my lips to his.

My mate moaned loudly as he grabbed my ass and lifted me up. Wrapping myself around his body, I thrust my dick against his jean-covered cock. I shivered when I felt his hand wander over the crack of my ass, ready to submit to him.

"My mate." He growled, licking my neck. "What is your name?"

"Trey Donovan." I panted as he pushed a finger against my hole. "I need you now, my mate. Claim me as yours."

"I'm Addison Cambell, little one," Addison said, squeezing my ass harder. "I have lube in my cruiser."

"Take me there and fuck me." I begged, feeling the desperate need to claim him and be claimed. "I have forty-eight hours to claim my mate from the time I smell him."

"That's different than wolves," he said, raising an eyebrow as he walked us away from the party. "We have the need to mate, but we can control it."

"Don't control it. We both know we're mates and I accept you willingly," I replied, staring into chocolate brown eyes. Addison was gorgeous and huge, being at least six five and three hundred pounds. He made me almost feel petite at my five nine and hundred and eighty pounds. But his light brown hair versus his shining dark brown eyes was what I felt most drawn to. "I give myself to you, body and soul, Addison."

"I always thought I'd claim my mate somewhere better than the ground." Addison grumbled before pushing me against his SUV and licking my lips. "I want you so badly, Trey. Will you forgive me, and I'll make love to you in our bed later?"

"Yes, yes, please just fuck me." I begged, nipping at his neck. "I'll be in honeymoon heat for days after I claim you. We can do it in your bed, and every surface of your house, my big wolf."

"Frank told me that the honeymoon heat was real after he met your brother, but I thought he was yanking my chain."

"He wasn't. I promise you that," I replied as he lowered me to my feet. He opened the door to his SUV, and I saw that it was a police cruiser. "You're a cop?"

"Yeah, is that a problem?" Addison looked over his shoulder at me, his eyebrows scrunched together. "The Sheriff's Department here is all pack. My older brother Frank is a deputy."

"No, I think it's sexy." I purred, reaching down to stroke my cock, loving that his eyes followed my hand. "Who doesn't love a man in uniform?"

"Oh, you're going to be the perfect mate for me," he replied with a huge grin. Addison closed the door to his SUV and held up the lube for me to see. I was on him in a flash, ripping his shirt off of him before I clawed off his jeans. "Glad to know I'm not the only impatient one here."

"Less talking, more stretching my ass for you," I said reaching for his cock. Once I felt it, I froze. The thing was massive! Taking a slow step back, I glanced down and saw the third leg he was packing. It had to be at least ten inches long and six inches in diameter. I could barely wrap my fingers all the way around it. "Lots of stretching me out if this is going to fit into me."

"You're not upset, are you?" He asked, not meeting my gaze. "I'll be gentle, I promise."

"Why would I be upset?" I answered, looking at him as if he'd just grown another head. "You've got the most beautiful cock I've ever seen."

"I've had people complain in the past that I was too big," Addison mumbled, still not looking at me. I took his face in my hands and turned his head towards me.

"I'm your mate, Addison. You're the perfect man for me in every way." I whispered against his lips. "I look forward to years of having that gorgeous cock in my ass as you make love to me in every way possible."

"Oh, god." He groaned, kissing me fiercely. The second we broke apart, I spun around and got on all fours for him, presenting my ass to him. I felt his warmth as he knelt behind me, rubbing my ass. Then I heard the lid of the lube snap close as his slick fingers started to caress my hole. "It's fucking hot the way you offer yourself up to me, Trey."

"I'm a cat. We're all about presenting ourselves for the taking," I said, moaning as he pushed a finger inside of me. "Besides, I'm a bottom at heart, except when I'm in heat and will need to claim you."

"Good, because I'm a top." He chuckled, rubbing his other hand up my back. "Of course, I'll more than willingly bottom when my mate needs me to. Your needs will always come first with me, Trey, I promise you that."

"Yes." I hissed when he slipped in a second finger, pushing back against his hand. "Hurry, Addison, please hurry."

"Okay, baby, almost there." Addison cooed, scissoring his fingers back and forth. I moaned loudly, letting my shoulders drop to the ground. Crying out in pleasure when he pushed in a third finger, I became frantic with need. My whole body started to shake as I felt the slight burn of being stretched. "God, Trey, I've never wanted someone as badly as I want you right now."

"Take me, Addison. I'm all yours, please just fuck me already," I said, almost whining. "Shove that gorgeous cock in me and bite me."

"I need to make sure you're stretched for me, my mate," he replied. I went to say something else, but ended up moaning wildly as he pushed in a fourth finger. Moments later I was ready, and he pulled his fingers out of my ass. As much as I wanted them back, I felt a thrill go through me as I felt his dick up against my hole. "Are you ready, Trey? Tell me you want me to claim you, my mate."

"Yes, Addison, please make me yours," I begged. The instant the words left my mouth, he pushed into me gently. "Oh, fuck, it's so good."

"Tell me if I hurt you, baby," he said, and I could hear the strain in his voice. My heart warmed at the knowledge that he was putting the concern of hurting me over his own need to fuck me like an animal. "I want our mating to be nothing but pleasurable."

"You feel amazing, Addison. I've never felt so full and needed." I panted, trying to control the need to thrust back against my mate's desire to be gentle with me. "I won't break, Addy. I'm stronger than I look. Please take me like you want to."

"What did you just call me?" he asked, freezing in mid-thrust.

"Addy. I'm sorry, isn't that short for Addison?" I answered as I looked over my shoulder at him, completely confused. "Do you not like that?"

"No one's ever called me that before," Addison replied, tilting his neck to stare at me. I felt the relief wash over me as he smiled widely. "I like it coming from you, baby. You, and only you, can call me Addy anytime you want to."

"Can I call you my big bad wolf, too?" I giggled, moving my hips to get his cock farther into me. "Or how about number one of two mates?"

"Two mates?" He gasped as he held my hips in place. "I'll have to share you?"

"We'll all share each other, Addy," I said gently, looking back at him again. "They'll be your mate, too. But yes, cat shifters always have two mates since we go into heat. I would have mentioned it, but I'm sorry, I assumed you knew."

"No, I didn't know that," Addy whispered, and I shook with fear when I saw the sadness in his eyes.

"Do you no longer want me?" I asked just as quietly, unable to keep the tears from forming in my eyes.

"No, baby, you're mine forever," he answered, leaning forward to kiss me. Addison inadvertently pushed his cock further into me, causing me to groan loudly. "I'm just not a fan of sharing, but we'll figure it out when the time comes, okay?"

"Okay, Addy." I purred as I relished in the feeling of his body surrounding me.

"Oh, god, it's fucking hot when you purr, Trey." He moaned, pushing the last inches into me. I purred again when he ran his hands down my chest and stomach as he kept his hips still. It seemed to snap his control as he pulled back out of me and thrust back in with more force.

"Harder, Addy, I need you to fuck me hard." I panted, pushing my hips back to meet his. I gasped at the feeling of his sac smacking mine; it sent shivers of pleasure down my spine. "It's been so long for me. I'm not going to last much longer."

"Come for me, my mate," Addy whispered as he ran his tongue over my neck. He picked up the pace of his thrusts as he took me hard and fast. I moaned like a wanton, loving how I stopped being able to tell where his body ended and mine started. After several more minutes of us fucking like the animals we were, Addy sank his canines in the nape of my neck.

"Fuck!" I screamed as my climax overwhelmed me. The pain of his bite instantly faded into vast pleasure like I'd never felt before. My cock erupted, covering the ground below me with spunk. Addison lifted his head and roared out his release, thrusting into me erratically. I felt his seed enter my body, and I felt the peace that came with mating.

"We didn't get a chance to talk much, Trey," Addison said, and I could hear the worry in his voice. "What do you do for a living? Can you even move here with me? Would you even want to?"

"Shh, my mate," I answered, turning my head to kiss him. "I'm an author. I can move anywhere I want, and I would love to live here with my mate. My brother lives here now, too, and my apartment is only a few hours away over the Wyoming border. So, yes, we have no issues, okay?"

"Thank god," he whispered, and I felt him relax against my body. "You're an author, huh? How cool is that?"

"Depends on if you like your mate being a gay erotic romance author," I said carefully, not sure how he'd react. I'd gotten a wide variety of reactions for people in the past, everything from thinking it's cool to me being a dirty porn writer.

"I think that's very hot." Addison moaned as I felt his cock getting hard in me again. "I'll help you work out any sex scene you ever get stuck on."

"Thank you," I whispered, feeling myself tear up again. "Some people I've dated have had problems with it. I'm so glad you don't."

"Hey, you're my mate," he replied as if that explained everything. And it did. We were fated to be perfect for each other. "I think it's friggin' cool that you're an author."

"Good. Now feed me before the honeymoon heat kicks in and I fuck you in my half and half form." I chuckled, starting to pull away from him. "I'd better go tell my family I found my mate and will be going home with him."

"I'd love to meet them, but someone shredded my clothes," Addison said with a moan as he pulled out of me. We both sat up and stared at each other before bursting out laughing. I gave him a quick kiss as we got to our feet.

"I'll be right back, my big wolf." I purred, rubbing up against him suggestively before jogging back to the party. Glancing back, I saw him leaning against the SUV watching me intently. I made sure to wiggle my ass at him as I kept going, loving the thrill of him staring after me.

"Whoa, someone smells like sex." My dad, Martin, chuckled as I slowed down and walked up to him. "Guess you found your mate?"

"One of them, yes," I answered with a wide smile. "He's Frank's younger brother and an officer of the town. So I'll be moving here, as you probably guessed."

"I'll let your dad and mother know," he said, reaching as if to hug me then stopped. "Sorry, I can't hug you when I smell what I smell."

"No worries, Dad." I giggled, standing on my tip toes to give him a peck on the cheek. "I'm going to grab my clothes and head back to his house before the honeymoon heat starts. I'll call you in a couple of days when we resurface to talk about getting my stuff, okay?"

"Sounds good, Trey," he answered with a nod. I smiled at him before turning and racing to get my stuff. It was rude to leave without saying good-bye to everyone, but I knew my dad would fill everyone in, and I wanted to get to my mate. Minutes later, I was hopping in the passenger's seat of Addison's cruiser, and we drove towards his house, our house, and our new life.

Chapter 2

The next morning, I was sitting on the window seat in the front room of Addison's house, waiting for him to get home. It had been ten minutes since he'd gotten the call from his boss, the Sheriff, interrupting our enjoyment of my honeymoon heat. Already I felt like I was going to overheat and claw my skin off. But I couldn't help smiling at how well things were going. It felt right to be with Addison and even in what was a strange home to me.

It was a cute, two bedroom cottage he was renting, much better than my little one bedroom apartment. I loved the way he'd decorated it, with minimal clutter. This was great since I hated clutter. The living room had two leather couches, both with a seat that had a built-in recliner. I could imagine us snuggled up on them for many nights to come.

I was also glad that he had a large master bedroom with its own bathroom. Though we'd need to talk about getting someplace bigger in the future when we met our other mate, it worked for now. Even the color scheme I liked, with every room being in various shades of gray or blue.

Noticing a cruiser turning into the driveway had me all excited, until I realized it wasn't Addison. A man about his size, who looked like family, got out of the SUV and walked up to the front door. I was grateful I had thought to dress instead of lounging around naked like I did at my place.

"I'm Frank," he called out as he got to the door, staring at me through the window. "Addison sent me to check up on you while he worked things out with our boss."

"Okay, be right there," I said back as I leapt up from the window seat. Opening the door after unlocking it, I stepped back to let Frank in. As soon as his scent hit me, I took several steps back farther. "Don't come too close. You smell too much like Addison, and I'm in honeymoon heat."

"Shit, I didn't even think of that." Frank chuckled, leaning against the door frame. "Addison shouldn't be too long. The Sheriff's pack thought saber-tooth tiger shifters were basically legend until we met you guys. I think he just wants to hear what Addison told him over the phone in person, so he can smell if my brother was lying to him."

"Fair enough," I replied, scratching my upper arms to try and remain calm. Frank's scent was different, but they were brothers so they had the similar scent of family, and that was close enough to send my body into overdrive. "Well, it's nice to meet you, even if I'm being totally rude and not shaking your hand."

"Don't even worry about," Frank said and then his facial expression changed to something serious. "Look, I'm glad he sent me over here, and we can get a chance to talk in private. There are a few things you need to know about Addison, Trey."

"Oh, like what?" I asked, raising an eyebrow. I was pretty sure I wasn't going to like where this conversation was going to go, but I had to hear Frank out.

"My brother is kind of messed up over his last relationship." He sighed, looking as uncomfortable as I felt. "The guy was a real dick and did a number on Addison."

"In what—" I started to ask, but Frank's cell phone went off and interrupted me.

"What's up?" Frank answered, obviously knowing the person. I watched the color drain from his face, and I felt the hair on the back of my neck stand up. Before he could even respond to them or tell me what was going on, I was racing to the door and nudging him out. "I'll be right there, Cord. Just try and keep them talking until I get there."

I closed the door behind us and raced to the passenger's seat as Frank did the same to the driver's side. Glancing at him over the hood of the SUV, I knew in my heart what was wrong.

"The hunters are there for Avery, aren't they?"

"How did you know?" he asked as we climbed in, and he threw the cruiser into reverse.

"I haven't a fucking clue, but sometimes I just know shit like that when it involves one of my brothers," I answered. Frank shrugged as he peeled out towards Ty and Cord's house, flipping on the lights and sirens. As soon as I'd heard my family was in trouble, every protective instinct came out, which overrode my honeymoon heat.

"All available units, we have a possible lead on the kidnappers of Avery Donovan." Frank said firmly into the radio unit and then rattled off the address we were heading to. I held on, trying not to panic as we got closer to my brother's house.

The minutes ticked by, feeling more like hours, before we whipped into the drive at their ranch. Frank hit the brakes so hard I almost ended up in the dashboard. Well, that's what I got for not wearing my fucking seatbelt. I jumped out and raced over toward the front porch where Avery lay bleeding on Ty's lap as three men lay dead on the front lawn.

"You're going to die, you piece of shit," the forth man spat out. He had several bullet holes in him and seemed to be healing like a shifter, but he didn't smell like one. I knew he wasn't a threat as Frank raced over to him.

"Avery, oh god, Avery," I cried out as I knelt beside Avery.

"How are you here?" he asked, eyebrows drawn together in confusion.

"I'll explain everything later, little bro. Just hang on," I answered. Cord came back with a large first aid kit. Everyone got to work on Avery as Frank held a gun to the forth guy, Jack. They seemed to be arguing.

"How could you do this to your own people?" Frank growled, shaking with anger. "Our council will deal with you if you fucking live."

"Boo fucking hoo," Jack spat out. Frank holstered his gun and pulled Jack up on his feet, cuffing him. "Just because I was born a wolf doesn't mean shifters are my people."

"Wolf?" Avery gasped as I worked on wiping away the blood on one of his wounds so I could see what the damage was.

"He's hiding his scent somehow," Frank answered him. Avery held up his hand for Frank to hang on to as he grabbed my shirt and yanked me down to him.

"That's the one that raped me," Avery whispered in my ear so no one else could hear. "Don't let him do it to anyone else."

"I promise, little brother," I answered, tears burning in my eyes. This motherfucker thought he could abuse someone in my family and come back to either take him back or kill him? Not in this goddamn lifetime.

I could feel the rage and had questions I wanted to ask Avery, but I just stood and did what Avery asked. I gave Frank a nod, who raised an eyebrow at me. I let my hand shift into a claw as I stalked toward Jack. I moved my paw under the man's sac and yanked upwards, slicing off his balls and dick.

"Rape someone now, you son of a bitch." I growled, wanting desperately to tear the man into pieces. Everyone stared at me with wide eyes as I spit in Jack's face. Frank didn't ask questions, just dragged a bleeding Jack to the police cruiser. Cord and Ty stared down at Avery, probably figuring out what he'd told me. Avery nodded at them, and I felt my heart break. I couldn't imagine the pain it caused Avery to tell his mates that the man who'd raped and tortured him for years had just tried to kill them all.

"Don't worry, his council won't let him live," I informed them as I knelt back by Avery. "I just gave him something to suffer through until then."

"Thanks, Trey." Avery hissed out as Cord extracted the bullet out of his side.

"Won't he heal from that?" Ty asked as he glanced up from working on Avery's chest.

"The wound will heal and close, but his dick won't grow back." I snickered as I pulled off my belt. I wrapped it around Avery's thigh and pulled it tightly. "He deserves worse, but we can't kill another shifter's kind without approval from their council. I mean, we can in a fight, but he was already caught."

"I would have released him again if I knew he was the one who raped Avery," Frank answered as he joined us again. "He can fucking bleed to death in the truck for all I care."

"Thanks, guys." Avery coughed as it looked like he was having trouble breathing. "He can't hurt me anymore."

"No, he can't, baby," Ty said as he pushed Avery's hair away from his face. "Promise me you'll hang on, Avery. We can't lose you."

"Fuck, I ain't going anywhere." Avery gasped. "I want more Belgium waffles and sex from my mates now that they've marked me as theirs."

"I'll make you waffles for every goddamn meal if you stay with us," Cord answered, tears running down his face. "I lost the only family I had before you and Ty. I won't lose any more. You fucking stay with us, Avery."

"He's already healing, Cord," I said gently, trying to keep them calm. I knew it had to be extra hard for them to see their mate injured and bleeding. It was killing me since it was my little brother, but I'd been around shifters my whole life and knew what we could heal from. "We need to get the last bullet out so he can shift and start healing."

"I got it," Ty exclaimed, removing it from Avery's thigh. I undid my belt and gave Avery a nod before helping him roll on his side. Avery screamed as I did, shifting as soon as he was in position. I felt the tears burning again as I caused that pain in my brother, but he needed to do it to help the healing. Avery shifted right back and I breathed again, knowing the process had started. No matter how bad he hurt, it was what was for the best.

"I love you, mates," Avery whispered before blacking out.

"Avery!" Cord screamed, staring down at him before turning to focus on me. "What the fuck did you do to him?"

"He needed to shift to jump start the healing." I explained, trying to remain calm even though the man was basically accusing me of hurting my own brother. "Avery couldn't shift while on his back like that into a four hundred pound tiger. I would never hurt my brother, Cord."

"We know that, Trey," Ty said gently, glancing between me and Cord. "We're just not used to how you guys heal and treat wounds."

"Baby, baby, please, you have to come back to us." Cord begged as he lifted Avery into his arms. "Please don't leave me, too, Avery. We need you."

"Cord. Cord!" I said louder the second time, trying to snap him out of it. When the man finally looked at me, I pointed to my brother. "He's just passed out from the pain, Cord. I promise you he'll heal from this. It just might take a couple of days, okay?"

"You can't know he'll heal from this!" Cord screamed causing all of us to flinch at his tone of voice.

"Yes, we can, Cord," Frank stated as he moved closer to his friend. "I've seen shifters re-grow limbs that have been hacked off, buddy. In a week, Avery will be back to new without a single scar."

"Promise me that." Cord ordered, his eyes darting between me and Frank. I didn't know what the fuck was going on with this guy, but I started to worry that this was the man my brother was mated to.

"I promise." Frank and I said at the same time. Cord stared at us for several moments before giving us a sharp nod.

"Come on, baby. I'm going to clean you up and then we're going to take a nap so you heal," Cord said softly as he stood. I watched in shock as Cord kept talking to my passed out brother as he kissed and nuzzled Avery's neck. I kept staring at the door they had gone through moments after they'd left before turning to Ty.

"Tell me I shouldn't be worried about his mental stability?" I growled, completely pissed off if this was the nut job fate handed my brother after all he'd been through. "I get he's worried about Avery, but that's not what a sane person does, Ty."

"I get why you're worried, Trey," Ty answered as he sat back on his butt. He ran his fingers through his head and then rubbed his face as I tried not to yell. "Cord lost his parents when he was really young, okay? He moved in with my family since he didn't have any of his own left.

"They had to go pick him up because he missed the bus for some reason and got into an accident, killed instantly. He shut down after that. Since meeting Avery, it's the most I've ever seen him remotely open back up. Cord's no more mentally unstable than the rest of us, but after that much loss in your life, you'd freak at the possibility of more, right?"

"Fair enough," I answered, trying to relax. "But you promise me that you'll call my parents and watch Cord. Don't you dare let something happen to my brother because he cracks, or so help me god, Ty."

"Cord might crack, but he'd never hurt Avery." Ty assured me as someone else pulled into the driveway. I glanced over my shoulder in time to see Addison jump out of the SUV and race towards us.

"Go take care of your mate," Frank said to Ty as Addison threw his arms around me. "We've got this."

"Baby, are you okay?" Addison asked me as he stepped back from me, eyeing me over as if looking for injuries. "What happened? Is that your blood?"

"I'm fine, Addy," I answered, reaching out to cup his cheek with my hand. "The hunters came back for Avery. He got shot several times, but we've patched him up. He'll be okay. I'm just a little shaken up. I just got my baby bro back, you know?"

"Yeah, I know," he said and then mashed his lips to mine. As quickly as my honeymoon heat had left me when Avery was in danger, it returned now that the danger was passed, and I was in Addy's arms.

"Addy, I need. God, do I need again." I whimpered, rubbing my erection against his thigh. "I was fine when I was worried about Avery. But now that you're here, and I'm smelling you, I need my mate so badly. Please, my big wolf?"

"You two go home before Trey mounts you right here." Frank chuckled as more people pulled in the drive. "Go. I've got my reinforcements."

"Thank you, Frank." I purred as Addison wrapped his arm around my waist and pulled me towards the SUV. "Please get me home and fuck me while I get clean."

"Only if you purr for me again, baby," he groaned as he squeezed my ass hard. "I love this sweet ass of yours."

"It's all yours, any time, any way you want it," I said adamantly as we got into the SUV. Leaning back in the seat, I buckled myself in and started to rub my hard on. I closed my eyes and tried to calm my breathing as Addison sped to get us home.

"Pull out that beautiful cock for me, baby." Addy moaned loudly, getting my attention. I opened my eyes and glanced at him as he kept looking from the road to where my hand was rubbing my groin. "Let me take the edge off for you."

"Okay." I purred, undoing my fly and pulling my dick out. Addy's hand was instantly on my cock, stroking me hard and fast. Without even meaning to, I felt my hips thrust up as if trying to help him get me off. "Oh, god, Addy. I love the way you touch me."

"Come for me, my mate." He growled, sending shivers down my spine. "I want to see you come all over my hand, baby."

"Fuck!" I cried out as my orgasm hit me. Normally, I had a little bit better control than this, but with my honeymoon heat, it was like I was always primed and ready to come. Wave after wave of pleasure hit me as my cock kept shooting more of my seed than I even thought possible. As soon as my climax was finally done, I collapsed in the seat, panting heavily.

"Watch me, baby." Addison said softly, and I opened my eyes to see him licking my cum off his hand. I groaned as he cleaned his hand off, taking long, leisurely swipes as he moaned at the taste. Instantly, I was getting hard again and wanting more attention.

"Are we home yet?" I whimpered, trying to calm down. "You can't tease me like that, Addy. I'm in heat and anything gets me horny again."

"We're home, Trey." He chuckled as I felt the SUV turn. Facing front, I saw we were pulling in his driveway, and I unbuckled my seatbelt. He barely stopped the SUV before I booked it out of the cruiser and raced for the front door. I hadn't even bothered to tuck my cock back in my pants, simply holding them up with one hand as I turned the doorknob. As soon as I was inside, I ran to the master bathroom and turned on the shower.

"Fucking clothes," I grumbled as I yanked them off. Ending up in the shower with my socks still on, I got them off and threw them out as I started to wash up. I barely had time to get myself stretched for Addison before he pounced on me and really showed me some water-time fun.

We came up for air long enough to call and check on Avery, who was thankfully doing fine. His outer wounds all healed, according to my mom, but he was still passed out. All lingering worry left me once I knew Mom was there and handling things. Though about my size, that woman could get anyone to do what she wanted with the raise of an eyebrow.

Addy and I did nothing but each other for the next twenty-four hours until my honeymoon heat passed. We did take the occasional "catnap," as he called them, totally teasing me. When we were finally done and able to get some real sleep, I found myself still awake as Addy snored softly next to me.

With everything that had happened, I never did get to finish talking to Frank. What was he going to have told me that was so important it was the first thing he wanted to tell me after meeting me?

Chapter 3

"Sasha, just box my shit up and quit bitching," I grumbled into the phone at my brother a few days later. "You're getting all the furniture and the apartment, for crying out loud. And I've already prepaid three months rent."

"I'm not bitching." Sasha snickered as I noticed Addison's phone vibrating. Something it seemed to do quite often. I saw him answer it and walk away out of the corner of my eye. "I'm just saying it's a *lot* of books, Trey. I just thought maybe you wouldn't want all of them at once considering everything else you're going to have to be unpacking and adjusting to."

"Good point." I sighed, rubbing my temples. As great as the sex was between us, the other areas of my relationship with Addison were sorely lacking. Case in point, these phone calls that he needed to always take away from me.

It wasn't like I was a jealous person, because I wasn't, never had been. But there were a few times already when I'd walk into the kitchen to grab something to drink, and Addison would be talking quietly into his phone. What really got me was the guilty look on his face, as if I'd caught him with his hand in the cookie jar. How could I not be curious or annoyed when he obviously didn't want me hearing whatever he was saying to whomever he was talking to?

"Trey, you there?" Sasha asked, drawing me back to the conversation.

"Yeah, sorry," I answered. "If you don't mind the books being there for a bit, you're right. Let's worry about those later."

"Good deal, bro. I'll see you tomorrow with your car and most of your stuff."

"Thanks," I said as we finished up, and I flipped my phone shut. I wanted to go find my mate and finally talk about the elephant in the room, but instead I made myself stay in the kitchen. I wasn't ready to ask him yet since I didn't know how to without sounding like a jealous boyfriend. I just didn't get it... why keep who he was talking to from me?

And that wasn't the only issue I was having with my mate. Last night, I had come up behind him as he was sitting on the couch with his laptop to snuggle his neck. He freaked out on me and snapped at me about snooping. I hadn't even glanced at what he was doing. I'd been focused on his gorgeous neck and the desire to kiss it. Needless to say, his reaction kind of killed the mood.

He'd apologized, saying he'd had issues with people being overly nosey in the past. But I hadn't been a happy camper. Again, it just made me feel like he was hiding things from me, and I didn't think that's the way we should be acting in a budding relationship. Part of me wanted to just say fuck it and go back to my apartment. I'd decided to be patient and give him some time to adjust instead. This couldn't have been easy on him either.

It felt like whatever issues he'd had in past relationships was leaking all over ours, and I didn't think that was fair. I mean, I was a different person than his ex-boyfriends. Why should I have to deal with the shit that they had caused with Addison? I wasn't the one who snooped or pried into his life. But I just didn't seem to know where the line was. When did it officially become too much to where I had to say something?

"Get everything straightened out with Sasha?" Addison asked as he came back into the kitchen now that he was done with his phone call. And it was a totally normal question to ask, except from someone who constantly kept everything secretive from me. Why did he get to ask questions about my phone calls when he took his in private?

"Yes, he and Kody will be bringing my car and most of my stuff tomorrow," I answered anyway. No reason to start problems when it was something that affected him as well. Sucking it up, I finally decided to ask the main question that was bugging me. "Who called while I was talking to Sasha?"

"Oh, my ex-boyfriend, Jeff," he replied, looking anywhere in the kitchen besides at me.

"I didn't know you guys still talked," I said slowly, trying to sound more casual than I felt. "How long ago did you guys break up?"

"Almost two months ago."

"I'm sorry. You want to run that by me again?" I asked, feeling my stomach falling to my feet. "You just got out of a relationship?"

"Umm, yeah," he replied as he opened the fridge and stuck his head in it. "What do you feel like for lunch?"

"Addison, don't brush me off like that," I said calmly. "Don't you think this is something I needed to know?"

"I don't see why. I mean, it's not like you don't have exes, too," Addison replied stiffly. And again I was hit by the fact that he kept himself and who he was from me. What was wrong with asking such a simple question about the ex-boyfriend he'd just broken up with and still talked to? "We're still friends. We talk and text every day."

"Every day?" I couldn't help but ask incredulously. "Why?"

"Because we like talking to each other," he answered looking at me like I was the crazy one. "So what? I'm friends with my ex."

"Did you break up with him?"

"No, he dumped me," Addison replied, looking equal parts uncomfortable and annoyed. I decided I'd had enough sharing time today and needed to process what he'd already told me. "What do you want to do about lunch?"

"I'm suddenly not hungry," I said quietly as I turned to leave the room. I knew there was a lot more going on than what Addison was telling me. As I headed back to the spare bedroom where his desk and computer were, the sinking feeling in my stomach started to get worse. Why would you talk to your ex-boyfriend every day after they dumped you?

The answer swiftly hit me, and I diverted to the bathroom. I made it in time to lose my breakfast, holding onto the toilet for dear life. When my stomach was emptied, I sat back on my heels and tried to catch my breath.

He's still in love with his ex-boyfriend. That's the part to all of this that's was missing. That's why he looked guilty every time I saw him on a covert phone call or his cell vibrated with a text. And Addison had been the one dumped, so that explained why I was taking the flack for whatever issues they'd had. He hadn't worked through them and made a clean break.

What had this Jeff guy done to Addison? The man was gorgeous and yet constantly picked on himself. At first, I had thought he was fishing for compliments, but then I realized he was scared that I didn't find him attractive. Sighing, I leaned forward to flush the toilet as I got to my feet. I washed out my mouth, then my hands and face as I tried to regain my composure.

There was another part to all this that was confusing me. If Jeff had been so critical of Addison that he had this horrible self esteem, why the fuck was he always correcting me? Most of the time it was stupid shit that made me want to roll my eyes. I couldn't see the reason that he actually felt the need to say something. Part of the time he pulled these statistics and facts out of his ass that made me just want to ask him where the fuck he'd heard that.

I headed to his desk and booted up the computer. I'd been out of the loop for almost a week now, and I cringed at the idea of how much I needed to catch up on. Opening my e-mail, sure enough, I had thousands of missed messages. I didn't need to reply to all of them, of course, but it was still time consuming scanning through them all to see which ones I needed to really read.

I found I could break up my e-mails into four groups. One, the junk e-mails that went out to everyone or really weren't directed at me. Two, e-mails I needed to read but not necessarily respond to. Three, the ones that I had to reply to and four, the crazy ass e-mails. Those were always my favorite. They could be crazy good or crazy bad, but they were always entertaining.

Sometimes they were as simple as excited fans who loved one of my books. They went on so fast I could barely keep up with what they were saying. Those I adored. The other crazy ones I didn't love. I'd gotten everything from asshole bible thumpers to people who wanted to meet me and show me what real sex was like. I always saved them just in case, but they made my skin crawl.

Next time I looked at the clock, several hours had passed. Rubbing my eyes, I stood and headed for the kitchen to get something to drink. My stomach was still in shambles from my earlier realization about Addison. Added to that, I was stressed out over the work I was now behind on. Five hours and all I gotten accomplished was sorting through my e-mails and deciding which could be deleted, which needed to be answered now, and those I could put off until tomorrow.

Again I walked into the kitchen and Addison was talking softly on his phone with his back to me. Needing something to settle my stomach, I grabbed a box of green tea, making sure to close the cabinet loudly. He jumped and spun around, looking guilty as he did every time this happened. And I felt my heart crush in my chest as I realized that over the week since we'd met, I already couldn't count the amount of times this had happened. How fucked up was that?

He walked out of the room as I got the tea kettle all set up. By the time it was whistling, Addison still wasn't back. So I made my tea, added some honey and grabbed an apple out of the fridge. Turning to head back to the spare room, I almost crashed into him as he stared at me.

"Sorry about that," he said, not letting me get by him.

"Save it," I replied as I ducked under his arm. I got a few feet before I glanced over my shoulder at him. "You know this is wrong, Addison. Otherwise you wouldn't look so guilty every time I walk into the room when you're talking to him."

"Trey, it's not like that," he started to say, but I'd had my fill and kept walking. I was also feeling betrayed, not because he still loved this Jeff guy but because when we mated, Addison swore to me that he'd put my needs first. And this wasn't what I needed, what *we* needed, for our blossoming relationship. If he didn't realize that soon, I'd end up resenting him. And didn't that just fucking suck for me?

* * * *

I ended up working through the night, returning e-mails, approving new cover designs, and updating my website. At about eight in the morning, I was finally responding to all my Facebook posts and messages. Next, I had two sets of edits that needed to be done right away. But first, it was time to switch to coffee since I had more work and my brothers were coming in a couple of hours.

"You never came to bed, baby." Addison whispered in my ear as he came up behind me as I walked into the kitchen. He slid his arms around my waist and pulled me back against him, his hard-on snuggling against my lower back. "I missed my mate being in my arms and getting my good morning kiss."

"I was working," I replied, pulling away from him. "I'm so far behind on everything, it's not even funny. I've not done anything work related since I've met you."

"It seems like you need some stress relief, Trey," he said. I shrugged my shoulders as I started making coffee. He tried again, this time reaching down to cup my groin as he kissed my neck. As much as I just wanted to give into him, I was tired and my emotions were fried from yesterday. I couldn't even get it up nor had any desire to right then. "Come on, baby. Let it all go so I can take care of my hot mate."

"Taking care of me isn't just about sex, Addy." I whispered, afraid if I spoke any louder, I'd start crying. The tears that had been burning my eyes finally fell as he stiffened up behind me. Without a word, he let me go and left the kitchen. My back felt cold, as did my heart, and not just from losing the warmth of his body against mine, but because of his mood. I finished making the coffee, barely able to see through the tears that were falling on the counter.

This wasn't the mating I'd always dreamed about, but I didn't see how to fix it. Addison's heart belonged to another, and no matter the pull we had to each other since we were mates, I couldn't change that. He had to, starting by making a clean break with Jeff. And I guess I didn't matter enough to Addison for him to do that.

Once I got my coffee and snagged a muffin, I went back to work. It took me over three hours to finish the first set of edits I'd had waiting in my inbox. And those were the second round of edits for one of the books coming out next month. Just as I was finishing up and thinking about taking a shower, the doorbell rang.

So much for that shower, I sighed as I jogged to the front door. I threw it open and, without even meaning to, launched myself into Sasha and Kody's arms.

"Hey, what's wrong, big brother?" Sasha asked gently as they rubbed my back.

"Nothing, I'm fine," I answered, pulling away. "Adapting to instantly changing my entire life is getting to me, I think. Sorry, you don't need to hear this shit when you've done all this for me."

"We're family, Trey. Brothers," Kody said as he yanked me back to him. "Your pain is our pain, you know this. If something's going on, you can tell us, okay?"

"I know that," I answered, rubbing my hands over my face when we parted. "I'm sorry, it's just I neglected work all week so now I was up all night trying to just catch up with e-mails and stuff. I'm just tired and a little frazzled by all the change, you know?"

"Yeah, being mated and moving in with someone suddenly would shake anyone up," Sasha answered carefully, but I could tell from his facial expressions he didn't believe me in the slightest. I wouldn't have believed me either, but now was not the time to discuss this, if ever.

"Hey, nice to finally meet some of Trey's family," Addison said warmly as I let me brothers into the house. They all shook hands, greeting each other as I put on my best smile. "Let's start bringing some of his stuff in, and then I'll make some lunch."

"Sounds like a plan," I replied, slipping my sneakers on. Part of me felt nauseous at the idea of moving more of myself and my life into Addison's house when we weren't doing well, but not doing it would make more of an issue of the situation. I decided to try the best I could. Kody tossed me the keys to my car, and I raced outside to see my baby. "I missed you, sweetheart!"

"You and that friggin' car." Kody chuckled as they followed me out. I didn't care. I was practically sprawled over the hood of my 2010 Dodge Charger that I'd saved like a madman to afford.

"Were they good to you, baby?" I cooed at the car playfully while sticking my tongue out at Kody. "Better have enjoyed getting to drive her. It's the only time that'll ever happen."

"We took turns just so we could both say we drove it." Sasha snickered as he opened the back of the small delivery truck I knew was from Sasha's business.

"You have a new Charger? Why didn't you tell me that?" Addison asked, looking at me like I'd kept the fact I was a shifter secret from him instead of not mentioning what car I drove. It pissed me off, especially since he did it in front of my brothers.

"You haven't been in the mood to talk. Well, at least to me, that is." I answered, not hiding my distaste at his comment by curling up my lip. He stood there looking at me for a moment before I could almost see the invisible walls slamming down around him. Great, so he could get more closed off? What the fuck had I been dealing with already?

Sasha and Kody seemed oblivious to what had just passed between me and my mate as they hopped up into the truck. I turned away from Addison to help them, taking the boxed they handed down to me.

"Let's put everything in the spare room until I can go through it all." I told my brothers, wondering if that was really how I felt or if part of me was planning to make that my office/bedroom. "We don't need to dump all my shit in Addison's room."

"Our room." He corrected me, and I just glanced at him a second before shaking my head and walking away. Our room? Who was he kidding? "It would be better if you put half in each room. That way, you're not overwhelmed by everything all at once when you walk into the spare room."

"Whatever," I replied, feeling just a little bit colder. Now my way of unpacking wasn't right? It probably seemed silly to let something so small affect me like this, but it was constant. He told me what type of toothpaste I should get, shampoo, toothbrush, coffee, and just about anything else I had already at his house. Makes a guy feel all warm and fuzzy when his mate picks at everything he does, says, or uses.

We moved over half of everything in fast since we had the added strength of being shifters. I grabbed my brothers some bottles of water as Addison started pulling out the fixings for sandwiches. Tossing one to Kody and Sasha, we all sat down to relax for a few minutes.

"Anyone have any preference on how they like their ham sandwiches?" Addison called out from the kitchen.

"We don't like fruit on ours," I answered, knowing exactly how my brothers liked to eat.

"Who puts fruit on a sandwich?" He asked as he came into the room, eyebrows drawn together.

"I was teasing about tomatoes," I said, smiling at him. I started to relax and try to move forward from our bickering.

"Tomatoes aren't fruit," he replied.

"Yes, they are. They have seeds," Sasha said, glancing between the two of us.

"Oh, right," Addison mumbled as he turned back towards the kitchen. And something just snapped in me. After all the times he's corrected me, saying I was wrong about something, and he wasn't going to say when he was?

"So that would make me...?" I asked, trailing off so he could fill it in.

"You were right, Trey," he said from the kitchen.

"And that would make you...?" I replied, doing the same thing.

"Forgetful," he answered with a laugh, and I felt my blood pressure rise. Addison could say I was wrong in front of my family, but not when he was? What kind of message was that telling them about the level of respect he had for me?

"I want to hear you say it, Addison," I said firmly, not backing down this time.

"Later," he replied, poking his head out from the kitchen so I could see the thoughtful look on his face.

"No. Now, Addison," I basically growled, ignoring the glances I was getting from my brothers. "You felt the need to tell me I was wrong in front of Kody and Sasha then you can admit when you are with them here too."

"Not going to happen, Trey." Addison chuckled, going back to the kitchen. So not only would he not do it, he found my point funny? I took a few deep breathes, trying to stay calm as I stood up and walked back out to the delivery truck. Again, I seemed to have lost my appetite. If this kept up, I'd be skin and bones within a few months.

Everyone left me alone as I moved boxes into the spare bedroom, deciding to do the unpacking my way after all. They ate quietly as I walked back and forth past them. I felt bad for making my brothers uncomfortable, but I couldn't just keep everything bottled in. Maybe Addison didn't even realize he was doing this to me?

"Are you seriously upset because I wouldn't say I was wrong?" He asked me as he followed me into the spare room.

"Not just that," I answered evenly, desperately trying not to yell. "You constantly correct me or tell me something I'm doing is wrong, and I should do it another way. And when it's just us, fine. I deal with it, even if I don't like hearing it all the time. But you just did it in front of my brothers, which pisses me off. If you felt the need to tell me I'm wrong in front of others, you can admit when you are in front of them as well."

"I'm sorry," he said after a few moments. "I didn't realize that I do that to you, and you're right."

"Okay, then," I replied, finally feeling as if we'd made some progress. "Then let's go back out by our guests and finish moving me in."

Addison nodded at me, and I gave him a quick kiss as I walked by him. He, in turn, grabbed my ass, and I laughed. Maybe things would work out after all?

Chapter 4

The next day I heard the front door close, signaling Addison was home from work. Getting up from the desk, I walked out of the room and over to him. I threw my arms around his neck and kissed him, until I realized he wasn't kissing me back.

"What's wrong, Addison?" I asked, pulling away from him. He wouldn't look at me, staring at the wall past my head.

"We need to talk, Trey," he answered quietly, and I felt my heart sink.

"Okay," I said, moving into the living room and took a seat. He sat down on the couch adjacent to the one I was on.

"I think we need to slow things down." Addison sighed, running his fingers through his short brown hair. "This is getting too serious, too fast, for me."

"What?" I gasped, a fierce pain in my chest. Was my mate breaking up with me? It's not like we could break the mating bond or be just friends.

"Look, I wasn't expecting things to progress this quickly or for us to get attached to each other like this." He explained, still not having the guts to look at me. "I just got out of a relationship and wasn't looking for another one. I'm not ready for another one."

"But we like each other, and we're mates," I stuttered, feeling as if my heart and soul were shutting down. "Why do you need to slow things down? Shouldn't you have thought of this sooner? Told me sooner?"

"Yeah, probably, but is there really a good time to tell you that I'm still in love with my ex-boyfriend?" he asked, finally glancing at me before looking back at the ground. "I love him. We ended things because we weren't what the other one needed, and he lives in another pack far away. But that doesn't mean I just stopped loving him because I met my mate."

I stood up, my entire body shaking with hurt and anger as I felt the need to shift swarm me. There was no way I'd even be able to fight it when I felt cornered and my place as his mate was threatened like this. I let it flow over me, not caring that my clothes shredded in the process. Addison stared at me with wide eyes as I roared out in emotional pain so loudly the windows shook.

The very sight of him made me sick, and I needed to get out of there so badly it wasn't even funny. Not giving a shit anymore, I leapt over the couch and barreled through the front door, shattering it to pieces. I didn't know I could cry in tiger form, but there I was, tears streaming down my face. I ran so hard, not even realizing where I was headed until I was turning into Avery's driveway.

Deciding it was better than ringing the door bell, I let out another loud roar to announce myself. Avery yanked open the front door as I reached it. I shifted back in a flash, collapsing into his arms, sobbing.

"He loves someone else," I wailed, barely registering when Cord and Ty came racing towards us from the barn. "My mate is in love with someone else and basically just gave me a dumping speech."

"What happened, Trey?" Ty asked as they joined us on the porch. I didn't see what Avery did as I buried my face into his shirt.

"They still talk, all the time. He tried hiding it from me, but I finally asked." I sobbed, shaking as Avery pulled me into the house. "He'd sneak off to a different part of the house and kept talking to someone. I didn't push him, figuring he'd tell me when he was ready. But it's constant, all the phone calls and text messages. And today he tells me that we need to slow things down since he loves his ex and wasn't ready for a new relationship."

"It's okay, Trey. We'll figure this out." Avery whispered, wiping away my tears as we sat down on their couch. I pretty much crawled into my little brother's lap. Not caring that he was even smaller than I, just needed the comfort. The doorbell rang in the background, and I found myself not even caring.

"We got a report of a large tiger running in this direction," I heard Frank say as he walked into the house. "Anyone care to explain that one to me?"

"It's *your* brother's fault," Avery yelled as he moved out from under me. I pulled my legs up to my chest and wrapped my arms around them, crying into my knees. "It seems he's still in love with his ex-boyfriend and wants to slow things down with his mate!"

"Aww, fuck." Frank groaned and I looked up at him then. He stared at me, such pity in his eyes that I realized that was what he was going to tell me the day we met. "I'm sorry, Trey."

"No, I'm sorry. I should have been more careful," I replied, trying to get my emotions under control. "When he told me, I completely lost it and shifted. I just needed to get out of there. The next thing I knew I was turning into Avery's driveway."

"Where is he?" I heard Addison call out from the front porch. Just hearing his voice made my blood run cold. "Where is my mate?"

"You're not fucking welcome here." Avery growled and while I was in pain, it made me feel somewhat better that someone loved me enough to put my needs first. "Get out of our house!"

"No, I want to see Trey," Addison said, pushing past Cord, who was blocking the front door. He saw me sitting in a ball on the couch, and I could see the indecision on his face. "Thank god, you're alright. You scared the shit out of me, baby."

"Don't call me that." I whispered, realizing what was about to happen.

"What did you say, Trey?" He asked, moving closer to me.

"I'm not your baby. Don't ever call me that again," I answered, unfolding myself and standing up to face him.

"You're a moron, Addison," Frank said, jumping into the mix. "People look their entire lives for their mates, and you've found yours. Instead of embracing him and loving him, you're wrapped up in this shit with your asshole ex-boyfriend! Your mate is in pain, crying because of what you've done."

"It's not like that," Addison replied as if desperate for us to understand. "Jeff and I are just friends now. I wouldn't cheat on my mate."

"It's not about cheating," Frank said, throwing his hands up in the air.

"But you are cheating," I stated firmly, getting everyone's attention. "It's not about having sex with him. It's an emotional cheating. You mated me and promised you'd put my needs first. And you're not even trying, Addison. You're so wrapped up in your ex that you're not even focused on us."

"There's no reason I can't still be friends with him." Addison growled, and I'm not sure why I was shocked that he was pissed off by this, but I was.

"I'm so fucking tired of your past relationship issues leaking all over me!" I shouted as I stalked right over to him. "Whatever he did to you has fucked you up. But instead of making a clean break from him and trying to build something with me, you're hiding it all from me. I didn't even know about him until I confronted you about all the phone calls. You barely talk to me unless we're fucking, but you've got the time to talk to him?

"And you throw me in the same bucket as him. I'm *not* Jeff! I'm my own person, and I've never mistreated you, Addison. I don't deserve this closed off attitude you have toward me. You were annoyed that I didn't tell you what kind of car I drive when I can't get you to talk to me about anything important. Oh, but you're always ready to yap away when you're criticizing me."

"I don't criticize you." He scoffed at me, and I just stared at him as if he grew a second head. "I just want to help you, like with the toothpaste."

"Here's the part you keep seeming to miss, Addison," I yelled loudly, my arms flaying around me. "When you say I should be using this kind of toothpaste, or this toothbrush is better for me, it's the same as saying what I've been using is wrong. It's the same goddamn thing. You're correcting me, telling me you know better than I do and that I'm wrong. Constantly. And the kicker of it all? Most of that shit is an opinion! It's not a fact. It's an opinion of someone who wrote something you read."

"No, it's a fact that pro-enamel toothpaste can—" he started to say, but I cut him off.

"I'm done. Get out," I said softly, looking right into his eyes. "You're so busy being right all the time and knowing more than me that you're never going to be my partner. You always know better. How I should structure my day, how to do edits, how to run my fan group. It's like me telling you I know more about arresting people. You're not an author. I am. I'm not a policeman. I don't know how to do your job better than you."

"Of course you don't," he replied raising an eyebrow as if he knew I had a point that he wasn't seeing.

"So why would you think you knew how to be an author better than I do?" I asked, crossing my arms over my chest. "You don't know how to do my job better than me, Addison. And every time you tell me I should handle something a different way with it, that's exactly what you're saying."

"Wait, is this about me still talking to Jeff or your inability to take constructive criticism?" He growled, shaking in anger.

"You wouldn't know what constructive criticism was if it bit you in the ass, Addison." I answered, shaking my head. "This is about you not giving us a chance and being my partner instead of treating me like I'm a child. And I'm older than you, to top it all off. You won't even try to move on from Jeff, and I won't be the one you turn to when you're just horny. You can't get your physical needs met with me and your emotional ones with him. I can't—I won't do that."

"I don't treat you like a child," he replied, but I held up my hand.

"You're not listening to me, and I'm done," I said as I pointed to the door. "I'll be by one day while you're at work to get my shit."

"Cord can go with you now to get a key from you, and Trey's laptop and car," Avery informed Addison as he nudged his mate, making it clear it wasn't up for debate.

"You're really just going to walk away from our relationship because of one fight?" Addison asked me, his eyes wide with shock.

"This isn't a relationship," I snorted, gesturing between the two of us. "This is a lie. It isn't real. And if you'd pull your head out of your ass long enough to see what you're doing with Jeff isn't allowing us to have a real relationship, you'd get that. And how much you want to bet that Jeff knows it to?"

"Oh yeah, Jeff would love the fact that he's screwing up Addison's mating," Frank said, rolling his eyes. "He doesn't want Addison, but Jeff wants him at his beck and call. And what Trey is saying that you're doing to him, brother, is exactly what that dickhead did to you. So shame on you. You don't deserve your mate."

"You don't know what you're talking about," Addison replied to Frank before turning back to me. "And if you want to walk away, it's your choice. But I didn't kick you out. You're the one ending this, Trey."

"No, you just gave me the dumping speech about needing time and space." I sneered, not willing to take the blame for this. "I'm not going to stick around while you only have sex with me and call that a relationship. I'd rather get out now than end up hating you for not being a true mate to me."

Addison opened his mouth to say something, but then snapped it shut. He turned on his heel and stormed out of the house as Cord followed him. As soon as I heard the car start and turn around in the driveway, I sunk to my knees and sobbed. I couldn't believe he'd really rather focus on the man that dumped him and the past than the future we could have had.

I felt Avery's arms encircle me and a second set that I guessed was Ty's. But then I wasn't sure when I felt another person hugging me. I guess Frank and Ty were trying to comfort me as well. I just didn't know who was who right then. I was falling into despair so deep that I felt myself shut down emotionally. The pain just got too much that suddenly it didn't hurt anymore and all I felt was numb.

"I'm sorry, Frank, but you smell like him," I said softly, backing away from all of them.

"Come on, let's get you set up in the guest room." Avery guided me gently out of the living room, and I stumbled along in a daze.

"Wait. I'll get a hotel room when Cord gets back with my car," I replied finally shaking myself. "I didn't come here to impose on you and your mates, Avery. I just needed to get out of there and wasn't thinking."

"You're not imposing." Avery waved me off as he opened one of the guest rooms door. "And I'm your brother. I'm glad you came to me. You're welcome to stay as long as you like."

"I need to find a place here." I sighed, collapsing on the bed with my head in my hands. "Sasha already moved into my apartment, and I don't think I should leave the area. I don't know what will happen when I go into heat in two weeks without my mate."

"We can deal with this tomorrow, Trey," Avery said gently as he pulled back the covers. I took the hint and crawled into bed. "You've been through enough today, okay? You need to rest, and we'll figure everything out later."

"I love you, baby bro," I replied, giving him a quick hug. He smiled at me and kissed my check before leaving the room, closing the door behind me. I didn't think I'd be able to sleep, but I was so tired that I was out the second I hit the pillow.

* * * *

I went through the motions the next couple of days in a fog. Addison never tried to even bother calling me or fighting for his mate. That, I think, hurt worse than anything else he'd done. He didn't even seem to fucking care that he'd hurt me or that our relationship was over before it really even started. He knew I'd be going into heat every month and that it was strong enough that fate gave cat shifters two mates.

Cord, Ty, Avery, and even Frank helped me move my stuff out of Addison's house once I found a place of my own to rent. It wasn't far from Avery's place, a few miles down the road from them on the outside of town.

The house came with a few acres of land, and it was bigger than Addison's place. But I'd given Sasha all my furniture, so I was pretty much sleeping on the floor. I'd thought I didn't need any of it, including all my plates, dishes, and glasses, since I'd been moving in with my mate.

When my back starting hurting so bad I was having trouble walking in the morning, I realized it was time to dip into my savings. I showered, dressed, and headed out to my car with the one goal of getting what I'd need to start my new life without my mate. Driving to Billings, I was there inside a half an hour.

I found a furniture store chain and pulled in the parking lot. As I walked around, I was having trouble really caring as to what I got. I walked over to the beds, knowing that it and a desk were the main priorities. Glancing them over I decided to get a nice big king size one. I laid down on the closest one and snuggled down into it. Closing my eyes, I tried to picture sleeping on this every night.

When the bed dipped next to me and his scent hit my nose, I realized my other mate had found me. I wanted to be happy, but it reminded me what I'd already lost. Would this mate not want me either?

"Well, hello there, little one," he said softly, reaching over to cup my cheek. I stared into his deep blue eyes, and my cock responded instantly. "Do you know who I am?"

"My mate," I whispered, rubbing my face into his hand and purring. "One of my mates."

"That's right. Kitties get two," he chuckled, moving closer to me. "Do you live around here, sweetheart?"

"About a half an hour away," I replied quietly wondering what cruel twist of fate would let me find him when I was this broken up over Addison. "How about you?"

"I packed up my truck and hit the road," he said, staring down at me with a smile. "I was tired of waiting for my mate to find me, so I decided to try and find him."

"You're from the south." I purred, loving his deep drawl as he spoke to me. "What's your name? I'm Trey Donovan."

"Jasper Knight, and yes, I'm from Texas, Trey," Jasper answered, leaning down to kiss me. Before he did, I turned my face away from his and felt tears burn in my eyes. "Who hurt you, little one?"

"My other mate didn't want me," I replied softly, unable to stop the pain in my chest. "I won't make the same mistakes he did. I need to tell you what happened before we go any further. And I wish with all my heart I'd met you first so I didn't bring this heartache into our mating."

"Shh, it's okay, sweetheart," Jasper cooed as he pulled me into his lap. "We'll figure this all out, okay? Let's start simple. Why are you in this furniture store?"

"I gave up my apartment and furniture to my brother when I met my mate since I was moving him with him," I explained, rubbing my head over his shoulder, wanting to mark my scent on him. "When I left, I stayed with my other brother a few days while I found a place of my own. Avery and his mates helped me move into my new house, but I don't have any furniture. My back hurts from sleeping on the floor, so I came shopping."

"I'm so glad you did, Trey," he whispered in my ear, sending shivers down my spine. "I smelled my mate's scent outside and followed it in here to find you."

"Have you recently gotten out of a complicated relationship or been dumped?" I blurted out, needing to know I wouldn't get crushed again. I stared up at him as my question registered, and he did a double take.

"No, I've never really been in a relationship," Jasper answered, and I felt his sadness at that fact. "Being gay in Texas can be a problem, so I had to keep it to casual flings and one-night stands. My pack doesn't accept homosexual members."

"That's horrible," I said, moving in his lap so I was straddling his legs. "I know the local pack doesn't have any problems with it."

"Well, that's a good think if I'm going to stay with my mate," he replied smiling at me. "If that's what you want?"

"You really want me as your mate?"

"Very much so, my little kitty." Jasper chuckled. "I've got some money saved. Not a lot, but enough for my plan to hop from pack to pack for several months trying to find my mate. So how about we get a bed? Or am I moving too fast after what happened to you?"

"No, not at all." I purred, unable to control it after hearing he wanted me. "Tigers are different than other cat shifters. We only have forty-eight hours from the time we smell our mates to claim them. Otherwise, we start getting sick and end up dying."

"We can't have that." Jasper gasped, his eyes going wide. "Let's get a bed and whatever else you need, and then you can claim me, okay?"

"Please don't hurt me," I whispered before I'd even realized I wanted to say it. Feeling embarrassed, I buried my face in his neck as he surprised me by hugging me tightly.

"I'll try my best, Trey," he said gently. "I'm new to this relationship thing, and I've not lived with anyone for years. But if I do something wrong or upset you, promise to tell me?"

"I promise, as long as you'll do the same with me," I replied, leaning back to look up at him. His blue eyes sparkled, and his smile made my heart skip a beat. Jasper had to be at least six six. I guessed since it was hard to tell when he was sitting down. He had light brown hair a little lighter than Addison's, but was just as built, maybe even more muscular. "You're gorgeous."

"I was thinking the same thing about you," Jasper said, giving me a wink as he stood and lowered me to my feet. "I've always had a thing for redheads."

"Is it too mushy that I want to buy the bed we met on?" I asked, not meeting his eyes as we still stood pressed together. I felt his hard cock twitch against me, giving me his answer.

"I think it's perfect, actually," he answered, leaning down to kiss me but then stopped. I wanted it, though I had to give him credit for controlling himself when he knew I'd been hurt.

"I want to kiss you, too," I said quietly, staring up at him. "I j–just need a little more time. Please don't be upset?"

"Never, sweetheart," Jasper replied with a smile as he cupped my cheek. "You take all the time you need, okay? I'm sorry your other mate hurt you, but I'm not him. I want you to be my mate, Trey. You're already more than I could ever have hoped for."

That was all I needed to hear. I stood up on my tiptoes and gently touched my lips to his. It was electric. I felt that kiss throughout my entire body. Throwing my arms around his neck, I melted against him. Jasper licked my lips, and I moaned as I opened up for him. The feeling of his tongue sliding over mine just about had me coming in my pants.

"Can I help you gentlemen?" a man asked, clearing his throat.

"Sorry, we were just excited to find our new bed for our new home," Jasper chuckled as we pulled apart. He moved us so we could face the salesman, pulling me back against his chest. I felt safe and wanted as he wrapped his arms around me. "We want this exact bed. Not just one like it, please."

"You want the display bed?" he asked, scrunching his eyebrows together. I nodded before smiling up at Jasper, who was doing the same. "Okay, then."

We ended up being able to finagle same day delivery for the bed, desk, and kitchen table set we picked out. The bedroom set, including two dressers, was at the store's warehouse, so it would get delivered tomorrow. Once we were done there, we decided to hit Target and get some other basics we could survive off of for now.

Chapter 5

"I feel like I'm overheating." I moaned, rubbing up against Jasper as we walked out of Target with our purchases. "It's like a combination of blue balls and sitting in a hot tub too long."

"What can I do to help, sweetheart?" he asked me as we got to my car. We'd taken it from the furniture store since Jasper's truck was already loaded to the max. I didn't answer him, only moaning as I rubbed my cock against his jean-covered thigh. "Be good, my little kitty. Otherwise, everyone here will get quite the show."

"I don't care, Jasper," I begged, pushing harder against him. Running my hands up his stomach and chest suggestively, I felt a thrill go through me when he shivered. We'd had so much fun simply hanging out and shopping, and it was nice to know he wanted me sexually, too. "Please, Jasper."

"What can I do, baby?" He groaned, looking concerned and turned on all at once.

"Load up the car as fast as you can and then break the speed limit to get to my house?" I asked, not sure what else we could do either. "I gave you the address and directions, right?"

"Yes," Jasper answered, taking the keys from me to unlock the trunk. A second later, he handed them right back and moved away from me. "You go start the car and try to stay calm while I handle this, okay?"

"Okay, my mate." I panted, moving farther away from him before jumping into the driver's seat. I didn't even realize I was doing it until I had my cock out and in my hand, stroking it furiously.

"Fuck me." Jasper gasped when he got in the car with me moments later. "That's a nice cock you've got there, baby."

"Please, please, Jasper, touch me!" I whimpered, begging him with my eyes. "I'm going into to heat and need to claim you. Maybe if we take the edge off, I can drive home."

"Okay, baby," he said as he leaned over to kiss me. I purred when I felt his hand on my dick, letting my own fall away as my mate touched me for the first time. "God, the purring is so fucking hot, Trey."

"I'll purr, moan, beg, or anything else you want to have you touch me," I replied, thrusting my hips up into his hand. He nipped my bottom lip then licked away the sting. I purred again when he kissed his way along my jaw and up to my ear. My ears were such a hot spot for me that the second he sucked on my right lobe, it set me off.

"That's it. Come for me, my little kitty." Jasper hissed in my ear as I came unglued. Biting my lip so I didn't scream and draw attention to us, my cock erupted in his hand. He stroked me harder through each wave of my orgasm until, finally, I was sated. I lay back against the seat like a wet noodle, panting heavily. "You are so beautiful, Trey."

"I'm so glad you think so," I said, smiling at him like a loon. He gently tucked me back into my pants after he found some napkins I had in the center console and cleaned us both up. "I want more, Jasper."

"I know, baby," he replied, looking at me with such lust I shivered. "I want it too. But let's get home first so I can explore every inch of your sexy little body."

"Oh, god, don't say things like that." I moaned, facing forward and starting the car. Checking to make sure no one was around, I threw it in reverse and got us back to the furniture store as quickly as I could. Jasper gave me a quick kiss before hopping out and getting in his own truck. He was going to make one quick stop to get supplies since neither of us had any, and we'd not thought of it at the store.

I drove home like a man with demons of Hell on his ass. The longer I was away from Jasper the hotter my skin got. I made the drive in twenty-five minutes, and by the time I pulled into my drive, I felt as if I was on fire. Barely getting the car into park and off, I leapt out and raced to the door. I got it unlocked, leaving it open for Jasper as I started to strip on the way to the shower.

Once there, I turned it on cold, full blast, and finished yanking off my clothes. The instant I was naked, I sat down on the floor of the shower and let the water cool me off. I pulled my knees to my chest and wrapped my arms around them, rocking myself as I tried to calm down.

"Trey? Why's the front door open, baby?" Jasper called out from the side door. My teeth were chattering so hard I couldn't even answer him. He must have heard the shower because moments later he stuck his head in the bathroom and gasped. "Fuck! Trey, what happened?"

"Overheated." I was able to chatter out. He pulled open the shower stall door and just about dove on the floor next to me on his knees. "I didn't know it would get this bad this fast."

"Didn't you go through this with your other mate?" He asked me gently as he reached up and turned off the shower. Jasper lifted me up into his arms, and I threw mine around his neck. "Jesus, you're freezing, baby."

"We didn't wait this long to mate," I answered him, feeling ashamed for some reason I couldn't understand. But I decided to lay all my cards out on the table. "We met at the party to celebrate my brother Avery's mating and his safe return to our family. Addison claimed me within minutes of our meeting on the ground by his police cruiser."

"Okay, let's not talk about this now," he said, and I could see the conflicting emotions playing across his face. I wasn't sure about all of them, but I could see sadness, then anger, and maybe jealousy. "Right now, I want it to be all about us."

"I'd like that." I purred as he grabbed a towel and started to dry me off. When he was done, I pulled his head down to mine and kissed him fiercely. On the way home, I'd decided to take the leap of faith with Jasper. I couldn't let my issues with Addison leak all over our relationship and not be the world's largest hypocrite after accusing Addison of doing the same thing. I needed to get past my gun-shyness and doubts and have some faith in my mate. "Claim me, Jasper."

"I don't want to rush you, Trey," he whispered against my lips as I felt him stiffen up. "I can give you all the time you need."

"You're not Addison," I said, repeating what he'd told me earlier. "You're my mate, and I want you, Jasper. Not just because everything in me is dying to claim you. But because I've had more fun today already with you than I can ever remember having on any date."

"I'm going to fall so hard for you, baby," he told me as he walked us out of the bathroom and to the stack of blankets I'd been using as a makeshift bed. "If you claim me first, will that help with what's happening to you?"

"I will go into what we call honeymoon heat," I explained as he gently laid me down. "We go into heat during the lunar cycle, but the honeymoon heat is the two days or so after claiming my mate. I will literally constantly need to fuck, suck, or be fucked almost the entire time. So I'll still be a horny kitty and in heat, but I won't feel like I'm getting sick at the same time."

"Then claim me, Trey," Jasper said as he sat back on his heels and pulled off his shirt. I purred as I got to see his wonderfully sculpted chest for the first time. Oh, and his abs. They were so defined without an ounce of fat on him. In a flash, I was on my hands and knees licking the lines of every muscle in his stomach. "Oh fuck, baby. Your tongue is like heaven."

"It's all yours, along with everything I have to give you, Jasper," I replied, staring up at him as I kissed along the top of his jeans. "I want to go slow, but I'm fighting so hard to stay in control here."

"Hey, we have all the time in the world to make love and explore," Jasper said firmly as he pulled me up against his chest and kissed me quickly. "Right now our animals are in the driver's seat. I'm just glad my mate is another shifter who understands that."

"Thank you." I whimpered as I yanked and pulled off the rest of his clothes quickly. He'd managed to get the lube out of his pocket before I tore his jeans off of him. As I pushed him onto his back, he handed it to me with a smile.

"I want you to know that you'll be my first, Trey," he said as he pulled his knees to his chest. The shock of what he said had me frozen in place.

"You're a virgin?"

"No, just never have been a bottom," Jasper answered, winking at me. "But for my little kitty, I'd do anything to make him happy or give him what he needs."

"I'll do everything I can to make sure you love it," I said as I leaned over to kiss him gently. "I'm a bottom mostly, but when I'm in heat I'll feel the pull to claim my mate, Jasper."

"I understand. I give myself to you willingly, my mate."

"All of you?" I asked, feel like an ass for still being scared, but I needed to hear him say it. "Do you give me more than just your body, Jasper?"

"You already have my heart, Trey," he answered me softly. "From the moment I held you in my arms, you touched my soul, and I gave you my heart."

"Thank you," I said, my eyes filling up with tears. "I'll protect it always."

"I know you will," Jasper replied as I popped open the lid of the lube and poured some on my hand. I dropped it on the floor after closing it, and I reached down and rubbed my fingers over his tight, pink hole. He growled his approval, and I felt my tiger go wild at the idea of our big wolf submitting to us. I pushed a finger into him, loving the way Jasper trusted me enough to relax and let me in. "What kind of kitty are you, Trey? You smell of cat, but I can't figure which."

"I'm a saber-tooth tiger," I answered, glancing up as his face as I slid a second finger in him. He gasped, nodding that he'd heard my answer. "You should see what I can do with my rough tongue."

"Oh, god, baby," he moaned, his knuckles going white on his legs. "Hurry, my mate."

"I don't want to hurt you, Jasper," I replied gently as I scissored my fingers back and forth.

"It seems I like the burn," Jasper panted. Deciding to speed things up, I grabbed his massive cock with my other hand and stroked him. I started purring, knowing it would drive him nuts as I pushed in a third finger. When he gasped in pain, I twisted my wrist and rubbed over his sweet spot. "Fuck! That's what it feels like to have someone rub your prostate?"

"I told you I'd make it good for you." I kept purring as I ran my thumb over the leaking slit of his cock.

"I'm ready, Trey. Please, I need you, baby." He begged, sending another thrill through my tiger. Quickly pulling my fingers free of him, I helped him roll over onto his hands and knees. I let the change flow over me so that I was in my half and half form. "Your fur tickles my ass."

"Is that a bad thing?" I asked, freezing in place with my dick lined up with his waiting hold.

"No, I love it," Jasper answered as he glanced at me over his shoulder. "Claim your mate, Trey. I submit to you willingly."

"Thank fuck," I said, pushing into him slowly. He gasped as I got a few inches into him. But when I started moving in shallow strokes to keep loosening him up, it turned into a moan. I had to still his hips with my clawed hands as he tried to push back and take more of me. "Go slow, Jasper."

"Don't wanna." He whimpered, looking at me again as he lowered his shoulders to the floor. "I want to be yours forever, Trey."

"You are, my big wolf." I purred, thrusting the rest of the way into him. We both cried out at the sensations racing through us at our first coupling. The moment I felt him relax enough for me to move, I started in long, slow thrusts. It took every ounce of my control not to fuck him into the floor while I licked and bit him, but Jasper was worth it.

"I think I'll want to not always top." Jasper panted, spurring my lust on. I snarled in approval, sounding more tiger than man. Holding onto his hips tighter, I tried to be careful of my claws as I started fucking him harder. I knew he'd have bruises, but I also felt a thrill go through me that I was marking him. "Trey! Give it to me, Trey!"

"Yes, my mate," I grunted, picking up the pace. His body shivered under me, letting me know he was getting close. I leaned over so I could lick his neck and changed the angle so I was hitting his sweet spot. Jasper moaned loudly, tilting his neck to give me better access. "Come for me, my big wolf."

"Trey!" He screamed as I sunk my teeth into his shoulder. Jasper came so hard I was worried the muscles in his ass might never let my cock go again. Not that I'd really complain about always being attached to my mate, but that would make life complicated. The taste of my mate's blood flowed over my taste buds, my tiger growling in approval at knowing that Jasper was really ours now.

I raised my head and roared out my release, pounding into Jasper like the animal I was as my cock shot streams of my seed into him. My body started to shake at the force of my orgasm, and I was having trouble staying upright as lights flashed behind my eyes. Just as it started to ebb, the knot came out and latched onto Jasper's prostate.

"What the fuck?" He gasped, looking at me over his shoulder.

"That's right. Wolves don't have a mating knot." I purred as I swirled my hips, having forgotten that fact.

"No, no we don't," Jasper moaned as his eyes rolled up into his head. He collapsed under me, and I barely moved my hands in time to brace my weight and not fall on him.

I chuckled as I looked over my gorgeous mate. He really was something else. I mean how many shifters were there that didn't have mates? Most waited their whole lives to find their other half. I know I had been. That thought made me sad again as images of Addison came to the front of my mind.

Shaking them away, my knot receded, and I gently pulled out of my mate. I rolled him so that he wasn't lying in his cooling spunk. My admiration for the man who'd packed up everything he owned and went in search for his mate instead of waiting from them to find him went even higher as I studied the peaceful look on his face. It touched me that he'd pushed down his own wolf's needs to give me what I needed to ease my discomfort.

I lifted him up over to one of the clean blankets and dragged him on it into the bathroom. Knowing the movers would be here soon, I'd decided it was best they didn't see my naked, passed out man. I washed him up gently, taking my time to make sure my mate was taken care of. When he was clean, I wrapped him in the blanket so he wouldn't be cold and grabbed a pillow for under his head.

Shifting back, I put his clothes in the bathroom with him as well. I pulled on my own and straightened up. Within a half an hour I had the new sheets in the washer so they didn't have that packaged smell. I had everything we'd bought from Target out of the car and put away. Well, except things like the new dishes and glasses. Those I had in the dishwasher. Just as I was finishing that up and wondering what we should do for lunch, I felt a warm body press up against me.

"I'll bottom for you any time, my little kitty," Jasper whispered as he nibbled my neck, his strong arms wrapping around me. "Thank you for taking such good care of me while I was passed out."

"Anything for my mate," I purred, pushing my ass back against his groin. He moaned and bit my neck harder. "I think it's time for you to claim me, don't you?"

"Do we have time before the movers?" he asked, and, as if right on cue, the doorbell rang. We both froze, then started laughing like loons. I was glad he'd thrown on his jeans at least as we headed to the front door. My tiger would be all kinds of pissed if other men saw what my mate was packing. Jasper opened the door, and we got out of the delivery men's way.

"Wow. I have so many questions racing through my head," I said after they brought in the bed. I was following Jasper out to his truck to help him unload before the next round of heat started for me. Part of me wanted to bring it on after the amazing sex we'd already had, but since we weren't alone, I'd opted against it.

"Ask me anything, Trey, I'm an open book to you," he replied as lowered the tail gate. Without even meaning to, I wrapped my arms around him from behind, hugging him fiercely.

"Thank you," I whispered, burying my face into his shirtless muscular back.

"Hey now, what's wrong?" Jasper asked gently as he turned around and hugged me, too. "I didn't mean to upset you, baby."

"No, it's good," I answered as I smiled up at him. "I'm grateful you're so willing to share everything with me, all of you."

"I did just let you take my ass, my little kitty," he said softly against my ear. His hot breath blowing across my neck and ear instantly got me rock hard. I jumped back and out of his arms before I did something bad.

"After the movers leave," I warned him, pushing the heel of my hand into my cock to try and get it to calm back down. "You have to be careful when kitty is in heat, Jasper."

"I'm sorry. I didn't mean to get you all wound up," Jasper replied, his cheeks turning a little pink. He winked at me and went to pick up some boxes. I groaned as he leaned over, his very firm ass pressing against his jeans as the muscles of his back rippled with his movements.

"I need another cold fucking shower," I grumbled as I took a couple of boxes and walked away. His laughter followed me into the house, and I couldn't help but crack a smile at the way Jasper made me feel so lighthearted again. It was a step in the right direction for my new life without Addison and with my other mate who actually wanted me. Now, if the movers would just fucking leave.

Chapter 6

After the delivery guys left, we'd raced to our room to break in the new bed. It was hot and amazing and hot! My big wolf fucked me twice in a row, barely taking a break in between rounds with that massive cock pounding in me. When we were finished, I felt like a bowl of limp linguini.

"Did I mention I really, really like the purring?" Jasper panted as he pulled me up against his chest. "It's like the sexiest fucking thing ever."

"I'm *so* glad you think so." I giggled, snuggling up to him. "I love the recovery time you have, Jasper."

"It pays to be young." He chuckled, and I felt myself go stiff. "What wrong?"

"How old are you?" I asked, tilting my neck so I could see his face.

"Twenty-four. Why? How old are you?" he replied, his eyebrows scrunching together.

"Shit," I groaned, moving to sit up. "You're just a pup!"

"Trey, you can't be any older than me," Jasper smirked as he sat up. "Come on, you're a hot little twink."

I felt my eyes get wide before I burst into peals of laughter. He just stared at me as I tried to get myself back under control. "I'm almost forty-five, Jasper."

"Ha ha, very funny," he said as he rolled off the bed. "Let's see your license."

"Okay," I replied, getting off the bed as well and retrieving it from my wallet that was in my discarded jeans. I walked over to him as he stared at me with wide eyes and handed it to him. He glanced down at it, doing a double take as he looked back up at me.

"You're seriously twenty years older than me?" Jasper asked, even if it wasn't much of a question as he was looking right at the proof. "Damn, you've aged well."

"Is it going to be a problem?" I whispered, twisting my hands together.

"No, my little kitty," he answered, his expression softening as he reached for me. I gladly went into his arms, hugging him back. Jasper ran his hands over my back, and I sighed against his firm chest. "Well, I've found out I like older men and being the bottom sometimes. It's been an enlightening day."

"I've got something else you'll like." I purred as I dropped to my knees. His cock instantly took notice of my face being so close. I pushed Jasper's thighs gently as he took the hint and sat back on the bed. Letting the change flow over me, I shifted to my half-man, half-tiger form. He stared down at me, raising an eyebrow in a way I found so sexy I got hard again. I moved to the edge of the bed in between his legs and licked the base of his cock.

"Oh, fuck, you're tongue is rough." He gasped, his eyes fluttering closed. I purred loudly again as I started to lick his cock like a popsicle. Jasper moaned loudly, bracing his hands behind him as he leaned back. It was so fucking hot to watch my mate open himself to me, to give himself over to me so completely. I took advantage of his position and wrapped my longer tiger tongue around him. "I think I might follow my little kitty around begging for his tiger tongue on me."

I switched off between moaning and purring, knowing the vibrations would do wonderful things to the dick I was lavishing on. It didn't take long for Jasper to get close, warning me when I felt his sac draw up. I didn't back off. Instead, I moved my tongue against him faster. He came with a cry of my name, shooting his load all over his gorgeous abs.

"That was fucking amazing, baby." Jasper groaned, falling back on the bed completely spent. "I–I've never experienced anything like it."

"Just wait until I rim you with my tongue," I said in between leisurely licks. His eyes went wide as he lifted his head to stare down at me. I made sure to take my time, purring as the taste of his cum hit my tongue.

"So fucking hot," he whispered as he cupped my face in his hand. "That might be one of the most erotic things I've ever seen."

"Something I can use for one of my books," I chuckled and then glanced up at his face quickly. I'd forgotten we'd not yet discussed what we did for a living.

"You're an author?" Jasper asked, raising his eyebrow again. I nodded and looked away. I squeaked when he moved to lift me up under my arms. Shifting back, I let him pull me towards him so I straddled his lap. "I think that's really cool, Trey. That's nothing to be embarrassed about."

"You don't know what kind of books I write yet," I said softly as I buried my face in his neck. Taking a deep, shaking breath I decided to just to spit it out. "I write gay erotic romance novels."

"Oh, that's hot, my little kitty." Jasper groaned, squeezing my ass firmly. "Will you use me for research?"

"You don't mind?" I asked, leaning back to look at his face. I was so shocked I knew my mouth was hanging open.

"What did he do to you to make you this unsure of yourself?" Jasper whispered, frowning at me. I tried to look away, but he reached out and held my chin so I had to stare at him. "I don't mind at all, Trey. I think it's hot that you write them, and I'm impressed. My mate is sexy, smart, loving, and everything I'd always hoped for."

"Thank you," I said, feeling my eyes burn with tears. "Addison didn't have a problem with it. Well, he said he didn't, but he was always telling me that I should do things differently. That I should handle my edits this way or do this with my Facebook page, like I didn't know what I was doing."

"Is Addison a writer too? I thought you said he was a policeman?"

"That's just it. He is. He's not an author," I answered. "Though he didn't have an outright problem with it like some people do, he's just very critical of everything I do. I've had some people freak out on me, so I stopped telling people. But you're my mate, and I want you to know all of me and be proud of me."

"Do you use your real name?" He asked, looking deep in thought.

"No, I use a pen name. Why?" I answered as I eyed him over, trying to figure out where this was going. Jasper's face lit up, and I swear I almost saw the light bulb go off over his head.

"You're T. D. Michaels, aren't you?" Jasper asked, his eyes going wide as he smiled at me.

"Yeah, how did you know that?"

"Well there aren't quite as many gay romance authors as mainstream," he answered slowly as he stood up. I slid down off of him, still confused as to what was going on. "And most authors use some variation of their own name, I hear. So I just put Trey Donovan together with the ones I know and figured it out."

"So you're cool with this?" I ask, following him as he suddenly left the room.

"That depends," Jasper said with a wink as he went into the spare bedroom and knelt by a box. I watched him tear off the tape, completely confused until I saw what was in it. "How do you feel about your mate being one of your fans?"

"My books?" I whispered, my eyes going wide as he pulled out the first books in the box. He kept unpacking the box until every one of my books that was available in paperback was on the floor. I met his eyes then, Jasper's wide smile warming my heart.

"I'm in your Yahoo Group, Trey," he chuckled as he gestured to the books. "I've read your stuff so many times that I know my favorite scenes almost by heart. The stories you tell are amazing, baby."

"You're cowboyjaz24?" I asked, my own light bulb going off as I put the pieces together. "You always post the nicest messages after I have a new book come out."

"See? That's proof I'm very okay with what you do," he replied as he stood back up. I immediately went into his arms. Jasper lifted me up, and I wrapped my arms and legs around him as I mashed my mouth to his. He moaned loudly as he squeezed my ass. "Everything's going to work out now, baby. I promise you, okay? Fate brought us together for a reason. You're perfect for me, as I hope I am for you."

"You're everything I've ever wanted," I whispered against his lips. I wanted him in me so badly, but my stomach chose right then to rumble and demand food. "I think your little kitty needs to be fed."

"I'll do more than just feed him if he purrs for me," Jasper said giving me a lecherous grin. I was more than happy to purr loudly for him, rubbing my face in his neck. He groaned as he walked us out of the spare bedroom and into the kitchen. The counter was cold on my ass as he sat me down on it. My heart was filled with such love for my mate already as I watched him move about the room to make me lunch.

"What do you do, Jasper?" I asked as he threw some sandwiches together for us. "I mean for like work?"

"I'm a horse trainer," he answered glancing up at me. "My parents died when I was a kid, and one of the pack members took me in. They raised me like one of their own kids, teaching me everything they knew about ranching and raising horses."

"You'll be able to do that here though, right?"

"Yeah, I'm sure there's need for a guy who's good with horses in Montana." Jasper chuckled, giving me a quick kiss before bringing our food over to the table. Just as I went to hop down off the counter, he beat me to it. I felt so incredibly special to him as he carried me over and gently put me down in one of the chairs. "I like carrying you, so deal with it."

"I wasn't complaining." I purred as he sat down next to me. "I love how big and strong my mate is."

"Good," he replied with a smile before we dug into lunch.

"After the honeymoon heat is over, I want to take you over to Avery's house," I said wanting to share my mate with my family. "He lives with his mates just down the road."

"I'd love to meet them," he replied then got a pensive look on his face. "I meant to ask you about him earlier. You mentioned something about being at a party to celebrate his mating and rescue. What did you mean by that?"

"Avery was captured when we were kids," I whispered, my food suddenly seeming like rocks in my stomach. I told Jasper the whole story about Avery being taken by the hunters and made to perform at that freak show circus. He wiped away a tear that fell from my eyes as I explained about the abuse my baby brother had suffered, but then he found his mates. "I'm the oldest of our litter, Jasper. I should have been able to protect him, or at least find him."

"Oh, baby, it's not your fault," Jasper said, and instantly I was on his lap.

I felt so safe, I finally did the one thing I'd not done since Avery had been found. I cried. I started to sob so hard against my mate, letting out all the pain of the years of not knowing what had happened to my brother. Then I cried in relief that Avery was finally safe and had loving mates. When I was finally done, I realized Jasper's strong arms held me the entire time.

"You needed to get that out, my little kitty." Jasper whispered in my ear as if he'd been able to read my thoughts. *"You can't keep things bottled up, Trey. It can damage the wonderful man you are."*

"Why can I hear you in my head, Jasper?" I asked, lifting my head to stare at him in shock. *"Can you hear me?"*

"Of course I can," he replied, looking confused and then really, really pissed off. "Addison never talked to you through your mental link?"

"No, what is it?"

"You know how you have the mating knot?" he asked, waiting until I nodded before continuing. "Wolves have a mating link with their mates. We can talk to our mates in our minds."

"That's so fucking cool," I said, smiling widely at him. But then I stopped when I felt the waves of anger coming off of him. "Why are you mad, Jasper?"

"Because Addison's an asshole." He growled, starting to shake with anger. "If you didn't know we could do this, he never did it with you. And that means he never really accepted your mating from the start. He had the perfect man and hurt him. It just pissed me off so fucking bad I want to tear his throat out."

"H–he didn't use it on purpose?" I asked, feeling part of me break. Addison had never even really given us a chance? He'd never even tried or wanted to be my mate, I finally realized, feeling cold. "Why didn't he want me?"

"I don't know, baby, but I want you," Jasper answered, his anger melting away. "We'll be just as happy without him, Trey. I'll love you as much as if you had two mates. I promise, baby. Please don't be sad."

"I'm sorry," I whispered, laying back against him. "I just don't know if it helps me feel better, knowing I didn't do anything wrong now for sure. Or hurts worse that he never had any intention of truly being my mate."

"Don't be sorry, Trey." Jasper peppered my face and neck with kisses as he spoke. "You have nothing to be sorry for, my little kitty. I'm just sorry you had to go through all this pain. And I don't know how to help you or make you smile again."

"Just love me, Jasper," I said softly as I licked the mating bite I'd given him. "Make love to me and show me how much you want me, my big wolf."

"Gladly," he growled, standing up and swinging me into his arms. I giggled as he ran back to our bedroom and threw me on the bed. He looked at me with such lust I felt myself shiver the seconds before he pounced.

Jasper took his time, exploring every inch of my body with his hands and tongue until I was a pile of lust-filled goo. Then he made love to me, really made love to me. It was gentle and slow and so incredibly intimate as we spoke through our mental link during it. We both had tears streaming down our cheeks by the time we climaxed together. It was perfect and exactly what I needed. Jasper was exactly what I needed. And I was falling in love with him, I realized, as we lay together wrapped around each other and fell asleep.

* * * *

"Are you guys home?" I asked Avery over the phone two days later after the honeymoon heat passed. "I have a surprise for you."

"Does it explain why I've not heard from you the past couple of days?" Avery asked, sighing heavily into the phone. "I'm trying to give you space, Trey. But you've been through a lot, and we've been worried sick."

"I'm sorry, I should have called," I answered, feeling like a schmuck. "I'll be right over, okay?"

"Good, you deserve a smack from me," Avery grumbled into the phone as he hung up. I stared at it and laughed. My baby brother was a fearsome creature sometimes, and I was grateful of it. After everything he'd been through, most men would have shriveled up and died, but not Avery.

"Everything okay?" Jasper asked as he came out of our bedroom. He looked nervously around the living room, at anything but me.

"They're going to love you, Jasper," I said, trying to calm his fears. I wanted to tell him that they'd love him as I did, but I still wasn't completely sure and held it back. He gave me a weak smile as I pulled him towards the front door. "It's just Avery and his mates. You're not meeting my parents and all my brothers at once like Cord and Ty had to."

"Thank god for that," Jasper mumbled as we left the house and got into my car. I held his hand as we drove over to my brother's house. As much as I hated to see my mate uncomfortable, it warmed my heart that he cared enough to be nervous. I saw Jasper go pale out of the corner of my eye as we pulled into the large ranch, and he saw the spread they lived at. "I can't provide for my mate like this."

"Hey, no one asked you to," I answered, and he jumped, probably not having meant to say it aloud. "We can provide for each other, okay? My books are starting to get more popular, and I have a good-sized royalty check coming at the end of the quarter, so we can get some more furniture. Taking care of your mate isn't just about the financial aspect, Jasper."

"Okay," he replied, staring out the window as I put the car in park. We both got out, and I immediately moved to his side, pulling him down for a kiss. He gave me a soft, but real, smile then as we walked towards the front door hand in hand. Avery opened it up, and I saw Ty and Cord standing behind my brother, protective as always.

"I guess I'll have to forgive you for not calling." Avery giggled as he pulled me into a hug. Then he pushed me inside the house and faced Jasper. "I should have said this to the asshole and maybe he would have treated my brother better. But I'm telling you this now… you hurt my brother or aren't a good mate, and I will slice your balls off. We clear?"

"Crystal clear," Jasper answered smiling widely at my little brother before giving me a wink. "I've thought about doing the same thing to Addison. I'm grateful to have found my mate and will do everything I can to make him happy."

"Good," Avery replied with a nod and stepped back. "Then welcome to our home and our family."

"I'm Ty, and this is our other mate, Cord," Ty said shaking Jasper's hand after everyone stopped laughing at Avery's outburst. Everyone had their introductions, and we made our way into their kitchen. It seemed no one knew what to say at first after what happened with my last mate.

"So guess who's a fan of my books and ends up being in my Yahoo Group?" I said with a wide smile as I winked at Jasper. He turned a little pink, and I felt my cock take notice at how cute he looked. "Jasper opened a box of his stuff, and there were all my books in print."

"That's great—wait, he's moved in with you already?" Cord started to say and then switched gears, narrowing his eyes at Jasper. "Do you think that's smart, Trey?"

"Look, I get that you're Trey's family, and I'm cool with that," Jasper yelled. He stopped himself and swallowed loudly, glancing at me before he continued. "I'm not Addison, okay? Trey and I have mated. We use our mating link and everything. I'm head over heels for my mate already."

"You moved in with your mates right away, Avery." I reminded my brother as I moved to sit in my mate's lap to give him comfort. Jasper immediately calmed down and wrapped his arms around me. "I'm not going to make Jasper suffer or pay for Addison's mistakes."

"You're right. We're sorry," Ty replied, always the peacemaker of the group. "Trey went through a lot, Jasper. You weren't here to see the damage Addison did to Trey."

"He's seen part of it," I whispered completely embarrassed that my mate had to deal with the aftermath of Addison betrayal. "And I'm so sorry for that, Jasper."

"You have nothing to be sorry for, my little kitty," he replied gently, hugging me tighter. "He hurt you, and you have a big heart. Of course, you were hurt. As much as I hate that he did this to you, I'm grateful that you have such a big heart."

"Well, that answers my concerns," Avery said as he took each of his mate's hands. "I just want my brother to be happy."

"I'm very happy with my big wolf," I replied firmly. Turning my head, I kissed Jasper to reassure him. "You guys want to hear how we met?"

"Of course," Cord answered, smiling at us. I knew he wanted to let me know that he was cool with Jasper now too. And I appreciated it.

"I'm from Texas originally," Jasper explained, nuzzling my neck. "I got tired of waiting for my mate to find me, so I saved up enough money to take a few months off and visit different packs. Imagine my surprise when I stop in Billings, Montana, where there's not even a pack, for lunch. I got out of my truck and smelled the most delicious scent ever. I followed it into this furniture store and saw the hottest man ever trying out a very large bed. I went over to him like I was in a trance, amazed that this beautiful creature was my mate."

"I went to go get some furniture for my new place," I said picking up the story. "I lay down on this bed, trying to test it out to see if I liked it. The bed dipped, and the scent of my mate hit me. I opened my eyes to see the most gorgeous big, blue eyes ever, and then this sexy man opened his mouth, and I heard his sweet southern drawl. He touched my cheek and said, *'Well, hello there, little one.'* And then we decided to buy the bed we met on."

"You think my drawl is sweet, baby?" Jasper asked, and I felt him get hard under my ass.

"Probably as much as you like it when I purr," I answered, wiggling on his lap. He bit his lip and stilled my hips as I snuggled back against his chest. I heard Avery giggle, and we turned back to them.

"I think that's so romantic," Avery said, smiling widely. "You should use it in one of your books."

"I've told Trey he can use me for research anytime he wants to," Jasper chuckled. Then he spoke in our mental link. *"Behave, my little kitty. Otherwise, your family will get a show."*

"Maybe you should punish me later, my big wolf?" And then I purred out loud, feeling Jasper get even harder under me. Ty cleared his throat, and we looked back at them, my cheeks heating up. "Sorry. We were talking."

"That's so cool you guys can talk in each other's minds," Avery said, and I was surprised he knew about it. He must have sensed my question because he explained. "Frank told us about that once."

"What's wrong, baby?" Jasper asked as I started to shake at the mention of Addison's brother.

"Shit, I'm sorry, Trey," Avery whispered, reaching over the kitchen table to take my hand. "You know Frank's a good guy. He's just as pissed at Addison as we are for what he did. If it's any consolation, Frank says Addison's a mess. Frank was here yesterday and told us that his brother's been on a bender."

"No, that doesn't make me feel any better," I answered, blinking back tears. Deciding to switch topics quickly, I was relieved when Jasper beat me to it.

"Do you guys know anyone who'd be looking for a horse trainer?" Jasper asked brightly as he squeezed me gently, letting me know he was there for me. "That's what I used to do in Texas and now that I've moved here, I need to start looking for a job."

"Actually, we do know someone," Ty said slowly as he shared a look with Cord. The other man glanced at Jasper again before giving a quick nod. I didn't know what was going on until I saw Avery smile widely. "We need one. We just bought the ranch that's on the south side of ours to expand, and the owner threw his horses into the deal. We've had a few horses since we were kids and know how to be around them."

"But with the expansion and getting fifty something new horses we're going to need help," Cord explained, looking mostly at me.

"We were discussing selling them since we're mostly cattle ranchers, but we got some great stock. Is that something you'd be interested in, Jasper?"

"That depends on what Trey says," Jasper answered, glancing from me to Cord. "You're his family, and I don't know how he'd feel about me working for his family. *It's up to you, my mate.*"

"You're my family now, Jasper." I didn't bother using out mental link, needing Jasper to understand. "That makes Avery, Cord, and Ty your family as well. I appreciate you wanting to talk to me about it. That's how mates should handle decisions in their lives. But this isn't about me deciding since it's my family. We're your family now."

"Thank you, my little kitty," Jasper whispered, hugging me tightly. "I'd like to see the horses and know what I'd be getting into before I decide. I also have references you can call and make sure that I'm what you're looking for."

"We'd appreciate that," Ty said smiling. It was then I was completely sure that I loved Jasper. He instantly and always was more concerned about me and my feelings than his own. And isn't that just the way it was supposed to be between mates?

Chapter 7

After we left Avery's, we went over to Alpha Daniel's house so Jasper could introduce himself and officially ask to move packs. The Alpha welcomed my mate with open arms and was thrilled that I'd met my other mate after the drama with Addison. I wanted to melt into the floor when I found out that the Alpha knew what had happened. He assured me that not everyone knew, but as Alpha it was his job to know when his pack members stepped out of line.

I started to relax until I noticed the way one of the Betas, Gregg, kept staring at me. When I asked him what was wrong, all the man told me is that he thought I looked familiar. It struck me as off, but then again some people were just a little weird.

A few days later, it was the beginning of the lunar cycle, and I made sure to take the time to get myself prepared. I had showered that morning and stretched myself, then put in a nice sized butt plug. As soon as I felt myself going into heat, I sought out my mate. When I couldn't find him, I decided to let him know that his little kitty needed him.

I'm naked, in heat, prepared for you, and sitting at my desk so you can fuck me on it was the text message I sent to his phone as I made my way to the spare room to check my e-mails. Less than ten minutes later, I heard Jasper's truck pull into the driveway. I assumed he had been over to Avery's to check out the new horses and smiled at the idea of him immediately leaving when he knew I was in heat.

"Oh baby," he groaned as he barreled into the spare room. I glanced at him over my shoulder and saw that he'd already been taking his clothes off. Closing my laptop and pushing it to the side of the large oak desk, I made a show of sitting on the desk facing him. I pulled my legs up so that my feet were flat on the desk as I stared at him and purred loudly. "I love you, Trey."

"What?" I gasped, my jaw just about hitting the floor as I looked at him.

"I love you," he said softly as he finished getting undressed. "I'm not sure if this is the right time to say it, but you're here and just so gorgeous, waiting for me, wanting me. How can I not totally love you? You're amazing and sweet, and so much fun that you're also my best friend, Trey. Just you doing this to mark our first lunar cycle together is wonderful."

"I wanted to make your fantasy of being my research for my books come true," I replied as I felt tears gather in my eyes. "I figured fucking me on my desk would get that point across."

"It does." Jasper nodded as he walked to me, standing between my legs. He reached down and wiggled the plug in my ass. "So does this, Trey. You thought ahead and prepared yourself for me. You're here purring like you know it makes me so fucking hot for you. You've thought of everything to make this my perfect fantasy, and I needed to you know that I love you."

"That makes this my perfect fantasy," I said reaching for him. He smiled and leaned forward, nestled between my legs as he kissed me passionately. "I love you, too, Jasper. I've never been this happy in my life, and it's all because of you."

"Thank god," he whispered, burying his head in my neck as he started to shake. "I was so scared that it was too soon to say it or that I was doing this wrong."

"It was perfect, my big wolf," I replied, wrapping my legs around him so our hard dicks rubbed together. We both moaned loudly as we mashed out mouths together. "Tell me how you want me, Jasper."

"You really are the perfect mate," he growled his approval as he pulled me off the desk. He flipped me over so my chest was down on the desk, my ass in the air as he ran his hands over it. "Can I really do as I've fantasized, Trey?"

"Of course." I purred, glancing at him I saw his face had turned a little pink again which gave me pause. "Well, I guess that depends what you have in mind, Jasper. We're not talking about beatings or sharing me, are we?"

"What? God, no, Trey," Jasper answered his eyes practically bugging out of his head. "I've always just fantasized about some dirty talk, and maybe a little spanking, baby. I'd never do anything to hurt you, I swear."

"A little spanking, huh?" I asked, purring at the end of it as I wiggled my ass under his hands. "I want to be your fantasy, Jasper."

"You are, my little kitty," he said as he leaned forward to kiss me. "Tell me if you don't like anything I do, and we can stop right away, okay?"

"I promise," I answered with a wink before getting into the mood of his fantasy. "I need a break from my writing, my big wolf. My characters are about to have sex in one of their offices, and I've never done that. How can I write about it then? Will you help me?"

"Gladly," Jasper growled, his eyes going wide as he realized what I was doing. I saw his cock start leaking copious amounts of pre-cum and knew he was completely into it. My body started to heat up as the smell of it hit me, and I purred loudly. His hand landed on my ass, and I gasped, the quick sting of it radiating out into pleasure. "That's it. Purr for me, baby. Show me how much you want my help. Purr and beg for it, my little kitty."

"Please, please, my big strong mate?" I begged and whimpered as he spanked me after each word. "I need my wolf to show how kinky my desk can make sex. Oh, god, spank me harder, Jasper."

"My baby likes that, does he?" he asked as he got a feral smile on his face. I had to admit asking for it harder wasn't because of his fantasy but because I really liked it. "Are you going to beg for my cock like this, baby?"

"Yes," I hissed, sticking my ass out farther for him. "Please, Jasper. Spank your bad little kitty before you fuck him into the desk. I want it so badly. I'm in heat. I need my mate."

"You want my cock in you, kitty?" Jasper replied, switching which side of my ass he smacked as he rubbed his cock against the plug. "How badly do you want it, Trey?"

"I'll do anything, Jasper." I purred, moaning when his hand landed on me again. I had a feeling I wouldn't be sitting down for the next few days, but it felt too good for me to care. "Whatever my mate wants, my big wolf. Please, please just shove your cock in me while you spank me."

"This is so fucking hot," he groaned as he pulled the plug out of me. I moaned loudly as I suddenly felt empty. "You want me to slam my hard cock in you, Trey?"

"Yes, fuck me, please," I cried out like a wanton, needing him inside of me more than I needed air. Then I had an idea of how to make this even kinkier for him. "Make me your little cock slut, Jasper. I want it so badly."

"Oh, fuck," Jasper moaned at my words as he thrust into me hard. That one thrust had him bottoming out inside of me, and we both cried out as the pleasure. "So you want to be my cock slut, huh?"

"Yes," I hissed, pushing back to meet his thrusts as I grabbed on to the edge of the desk. "Fuck, Jasper, I'm so full!"

"Bad slut." He grunted as he shoved his dick hard into me as he slapped my ass. "You're not begging for my cock."

"Please, give me that huge cock of yours," I whimpered more than willing to play along and beg for what I wanted. "Fuck me so hard I can't walk for days."

"If that's what my little cock slut wants." Jasper growled as he moved his hands onto my shoulders for better leverage. He started thrusting into me so hard and fast that the desk started groaning. "Purr for me. I want to hear you purr, beg, and then scream as you come, baby."

"More, Jasper. I need more," I begged, tilting my neck so it was exposed to him. That seemed to push him over the edge as my big wolf fucked me like an animal. I purred when I could get enough air under his onslaught of pounding my ass. He licked the side of my neck, growling when I shivered. I screamed when he sank his teeth into me, coming all over the desk.

Jasper pulled the cheeks of my ass apart and squeezed hard as he kept thrusting even though my ass muscles were clamping down on his massive cock. I felt him stiffen behind me as waves of my orgasm still hit me, roaring out my name as he came. My hip bones started to hurt as they banged into the side of the desk until finally my mate was completely spent and collapsed on top of me.

"That was so fucking hot." I purred a few minutes later when I'd finally caught my breath. I knew I would heal fast enough to not hurt tomorrow and part of me was sad at that. This was something I wanted to see the marks from to remind me how I felt as my wolf went all caveman and animal on me.

"Was I too rough, baby?" Jasper asked as he pulled out of me. "I didn't mean to hurt you or get so kinky."

"You didn't hurt me, and don't ever apologize for anything kinky that makes me come that hard," I answered as I moved off the desk. Turning to face him, I saw how his eyes had been staring at my ass. I purred loudly, and his gaze darted up to my eyes. "You liked that you marked me like that, didn't you?"

"I fucking loved it." He groaned as he sat down on the chair, pulling me onto his lap. I gasped as my ass hit his thighs. Jasper looked so concerned that I couldn't help but giggle before nipping his lower lip.

"I love you, Jasper," I said softly as I threw my arms around his neck. "Thank you for sharing your fantasies with me. We're going to have to play cock slut again."

"You really liked it?" Jasper asked, leaning back in the chair so he could look at me. I smiled widely and nodded, letting out another purr. "This isn't something I'd want to do every day."

"But it's something fun for when I'm in heat." I finished for him. He searched my face for a few moments before smiling and nodding.

"I love my little kitty so much," he whispered as he pulled me back to him.

"I think I should ride you like this next time we play and you spank me," I said, smiling into his neck when he let out a loud groan. It thrilled me down to my toes that I could get that kind of response from him after we'd just had such mind-blowing sex. Jasper really was the perfect mate and man for me.

* * * *

The next night at dusk, Jasper and I were taking a nap in between rounds since I was still in heat when someone started banging on the front door. I shot out of the bed ready to shift in a second. Glancing over at my mate, I saw he'd done the same.

"I want my tiger!" Someone shouted before banging on the door, and I felt myself go cold when I recognized who it was. "I want my mate. It's the full moon and I need my mate!"

"Is that---" Jasper asked, looking at me with wide eyes. I nodded as I tried to steel my emotions before going to deal with my other mate. Yanking on some shorts, I headed toward the door as Jasper came as well.

"I know you're in there, Trey. Your car's parked in front of the garage," Addison shouted as he kept pounding on the door. I smelled the alcohol pouring off of him when I got within five feet of the door. "You're in heat, and you're my mate."

"And you're drunk," I growled after I'd opened the door. "Go home, Addison. You made it perfectly clear how much you wanted your mate. I can't believe you came here drunk when you knew I'd be in heat for a fucking booty call."

"I want my mate," Addison whispered staring at me with tears in his eyes before his head snapped up. He growled loudly, shaking as if he was going to shift as he stared past me at Jasper. "Who is he? Already fucking replaced me, Trey?"

"That's my other mate. The one who actually wants me," I yelled, shoving him hard. Addison stumbled a couple of steps on the front porch before he recovered. "You're drunk. Go home, Addy."

I closed my eyes as pain washed over me at the slip of using my nickname for him. In a flash, I was in his arms with his mouth pressed against mine. "See, you still want me, Trey. You called me Addy. I'm your Addy, your mate."

"No, you're not," I whispered as I pulled back out of his arms. "You didn't even use the mating link you had with me. You didn't even *tell* me about it, Addison."

"I–I wasn't ready," he said softly before getting angry again when Jasper pulled me back against his chest. "You didn't have to move in with someone else."

"I'm his mate," Jasper snarled, and I saw this going downhill real fast. I tried to get Jasper back in the house, but Addison grabbed my arm and yanked me towards him. That's all it took to set the situation off.

Jasper moved around me in a flash and removed Addison's hand from me. Addison drew back his fist to hit Jasper, but since he was drunk, Jasper ducked easily. Jasper landed a nice punch on Addison's jaw, and he grabbed Jasper as he started to fall, throwing him off the porch.

"Stop this!" I yelled, trying to get their attention as my heart broke. They were mates, too, and there they were fighting over me. Or, I guess, fighting because of what Addison did to me. I wasn't really sure right then. They rolled around on the ground, trading shots at each other until I snapped. Shifting into my tiger and shredding my shorts, I leapt off the porch and crashed into them. Addison and Jasper fell away from each other with a grunt as they landed on their backs.

I roared down at them, a front paw on each of their chests as two sets of eyes went wide, staring up at me. They went to move, but I held them in place. They might have been shifters, but they were in human form right then, and I was a four hundred pound tiger. When I finally felt both of them calm down, I shifted back and knelt between them, leaving my hands on their chests.

"You guys are mates, too," I whispered, feeling the tears burn in my eyes. "We're all mates. This isn't how it's supposed to happen."

"I'm sorry," Addison replied, seeming sober now. "I started drinking to try and take the edge off my need to reclaim my mate. I didn't mean to get piss ass drunk and show up at your door. I was going to handle this better. I swear I wanted to. Seeing him set me off, and I got jealous. I'm sorry, Trey."

"I lost my temper when he grabbed you," Jasper said reaching out to cup my cheek. "I'm sorry, baby. I should have controlled myself better, but it's the full moon tonight. I know I've already reclaimed you, but everything is screaming in me that you're mine."

"I know, Jasper," I replied softly, nodding at him before turning back to Addison. "I didn't know the lunar cycle affected wolves sexually, like cats."

It was actually Jasper who explained as Addison simply lay there blushing as he stared at me.

"The urge to reclaim and mark our mates is unimaginable, Trey," Jasper said, glancing at Addison. "We're all Alpha male and dominating when it's the full moon. If I'd been thinking with the head on my shoulders, I would have realized Addison would show up. I'm actually surprised he didn't yesterday."

"I don't deserve to have my pain alleviated," Addison whispered as his eyes filled with tears. "I betrayed my mate and broke my promise to him to put his needs first."

I heard what Addison said, but I wasn't sure I was buying it. I turned back to Jasper as I sat back on my heels. Remembering I was the only one naked, I covered my groin with my hands. I had to give Addison some credit that he hadn't be staring at my cock. He'd been looking into my eyes the whole times.

"It's painful if you don't reclaim your mate?" I asked Jasper after a few moments of thinking. He glanced at Addison, looking conflicted before sighing.

"Yeah, it is. He's got to be ready to claw off his skin," Jasper admitted as he rubbed my knee. "Think of how you felt when I found you in the shower. Then imagine if I'd left you like that for another day or so."

I felt my eyes go wide at the realization of the discomfort Addison had been going through. Closing my eyes, I knew in my heart that there was no way I could let my mate suffer like that, even after what he'd done to me. Addison may have broken his promise to me, but I'd made the same one to him. And if I didn't do this for him, put his needs before my own, I'd be just as wrong as he'd been.

"Okay," I whispered, opening my eyes.

"What?" They both gasped.

"I'm sorry, Jasper," I said answering him first. "I love you, and as much as I don't want to hurt you, I made a promise to Addison. He may have broken his to me, but I can't leave him here to suffer like that. Not when I pledged to put his needs above my own. Can you understand that?"

"Don't do this, Trey," Jasper whispered as his eyes filled with tears. "I love you. I'm your mate. I've never hurt you. You're my little kitty."

"You said you loved me because of my big heart," I replied as I cupped his cheek. I waited until he nodded, knowing where I was going with this. "Would I really be that man you love if I let my other mate be in pain when I could help him?"

"No," he said as he pulled away and stood up. I went to do the same, but he held up a hand and I froze. "I get why you have to do this, Trey. But that doesn't mean I have to like it or watch him have you after what he's done to you."

"I'm sorry, Jasper," I replied, not knowing if there was anything else to say.

"I know, baby." Jasper nodded and took a few steps before stopping and looking over his shoulder at me. "I'll be in our bed waiting for you when you're done."

"I didn't come here to mess up things with your other mate, Trey," Addison said as I watched my other mate walk away. "Hell, I didn't even know about him."

"I won't break my promise to you, Addison," I replied as I moved to get on all fours. "Reclaim me."

"This isn't how I wanted it," he whispered as he sat up shaking. "I don't just want to reclaim you tonight, Trey. I want my mate."

"This is all I have to give you," I said, shaking my head. "Please, Addison, let's just do this, okay? I can't watch you be in pain, but that doesn't mean things are okay between us."

"Is there anything I can ever do to fix this?" he asked as he pulled off his clothes. I saw he was still shaking, and I realized he was holding himself in check. Again, I had to give him credit for that. I knew how I got when I was in heat and needed to claim my mate, and there was no way I'd be this rational.

"I don't know, Addison," I answered honestly as he moved behind me. He ran his hands over my ass, and I started to get hard. But the moment I did, images and words came back to the surface of how he'd hurt me. It made me lose my erection it was so painful. "I'm in heat, so we've been busy. You won't have to stretch me."

"Good to know," Addison growled as he pulled a small bottle of lube out of his back pocket of his discarded jeans.

"What do you want from me, Addison?" I asked, not keeping the venom out of my voice even as my eyes started to tear up. "I'm here, okay? You need me, and I'm here."

"You're right. I'm sorry," he said softly. I felt his now slick cock pushing against my hole. "Are you sure you can do this, Trey?"

"No," I answered honestly and thrust my hips back, impaling myself onto his dick. I knew I got about half of it into my ass as Addison moaned loudly. The rest of his concerns were gone then, along with his control. He grabbed my hips and thrust the rest of the way in me. I hung my head down in shame as the man who didn't want me took my ass. I knew I really didn't have a reason to feel that way; I was doing what was right by my mate. But you can't always help the way you feel.

"I've missed you so much, Trey," Addison said as he pounded into my ass. He still shook, and I knew he was still holding back from how he wanted to fuck me. As much as I appreciated that, I just wanted this to be over with. "I'm sorry for everything I did, baby."

I didn't answer, because I wasn't sure I believed him. And calling him a liar seemed wrong considering he was buried balls deep in me. Addison kept apologizing as he took me. My body and brain kept fighting against each other. My body wanted to respond to my mate being inside of me again. My brain kept reminding me of the pain Addison had caused me.

"Come for me, Trey." He grunted, and I knew he was getting close. Instead of pretending I was even hard, I tilted my neck, exposing it to him. Addison moaned loudly as he leaned over to lick my neck. "I want my mate to come first."

"Just finish it, Addison," I whispered as I pushed my hips back against his. "Please, just claim me."

He did as I asked, sinking his teeth into my neck. Moments later he lifted his head, crying out my name as he came inside of me. As soon as he started to come down from his orgasm, I went to pull away. Addison wrapped his arms around me and pulled me back against his chest. Before I could stop him, he reached down and went to stroke my soft dick.

"You couldn't even get hard for me?" he asked, disgust in his voice. That was it! I completely snapped. Elbowing him hard in the chest, he let me go enough that I could pull away from him. I whipped around to face him, seeing he was angry at my lack of interest in him.

"It's difficult to get it up when I didn't know if you were thinking about me or Jeff as your cock was in me," I shouted as I stood up. Addison turned his head as if I'd slapped him. "I did this to help you, and you're pissed at me because I wasn't begging for it?"

"No, yes, no," he said quickly as he stood up and moved towards me. He stopped as I took a step back and ran his fingers through his hair, pulling on it in frustration. "No, I didn't expect you to be begging for it. Yes, I'm grateful that you did this for me. And, yes, I'd like it if my mate was enjoying the sex as much as I did. But, no, I wasn't thinking about Jeff. I've never thought about someone else when we've been together, Trey."

"You'd just rather talk to him than me," I whispered, looking away from him.

"No, I don't even want that anymore," Addison said as he reached out and touched my cheek. "You were right about him. Hell, everyone was, and I was the only one who couldn't see it."

"What are you saying?" I asked, turning to him again as I narrowed my eyes. "You aren't talking with him anymore?"

"Not since the night you left," Addison answered shaking his head. "I called to tell him what happened and ask his advice on what to do and how to win you back. He said I was better off without you and that I still had him and that's all I needed. And it was like someone hit me upside the head, and I could finally see who he was. And then Frank came over the next day and basically kicked my ass."

"I didn't ask him to do that," I said, not wanting to look at Addison, but needing to so I could see if he was telling the truth.

"I know that, Trey," he replied as he ran his thumb over my cheek. "I've not talked to Jeff since, and I don't want to ever again. But that wasn't enough to fix what I broke. I've been trying to figure things out and get myself together before I came to you and begged you to take me back. I'm sorry I was such an ass and hurt you, baby. I don't deserve your forgiveness. I know that. But if you'll give me another chance, I'll spend the rest of my life proving to you that I mean it. It was never about not wanting you. I was fucked up and not ready."

"What are you asking for, Addison?" I asked as I stepped away from him and towards the house. I couldn't think with him touching me so gently.

"I'm asking for another chance to be your mate," he answered as tears flowed down his cheeks. "I miss you, Trey. I miss holding you and goofing around with you while we make breakfast together. I look around my house, and it just seems so empty without you. I can't promise that I won't fuck up again, but I'll try my damndest if you'll let me."

"I don't know if I can," I said before I finally listened to my instincts and ran. Addison didn't try to stop me as I booked it into the house, closing the door behind me. I felt like a whore as I raced past Jasper, who was lying in our bed, and went into the bathroom. Turning on the water of the shower to as hot as I could stand it, I started scrubbing myself as I cried.

I knew I wasn't a whore. I'd never been the type to sleep around or cheat. But it's how I felt for letting Addison have me when Jasper was the one I loved. I fell to my knees sobbing as I kept scrubbing my body everywhere Addison had touched.

"No! No, don't touch me. I'm dirty," I cried out when strong arms wrapped around me from behind. I pushed at Jasper's arm as I spun around to face him. "I don't deserve you. You can't want to touch me after what I did. I betrayed you and hurt you to ease his pain!"

"I love you, Trey," Jasper said firmly as he took the soap from me and pulled me into his arms. "I love you, my little kitty. You didn't betray me. Addison's your mate too. You did what you promised to do for him."

"How can you sit here and comfort me after what I just did?" I sobbed, burying my face in his neck. "How can you still love me?"

"Easily, baby. Very easily," he whispered as he rubbed my back. Jasper must have adjusted the water because suddenly it didn't feel like it was scalding my skin. "We'll figure this out, Trey. You didn't betray me. I mean that. You didn't go out behind my back and just fuck someone. You let your mate reclaim you when he was dying with need. It's not the same thing."

"I love you, Jasper," I wailed as I held onto his arms with everything I had in me. "I'm so fucking sorry. I didn't know what else to do. I couldn't not help him, but I don't know how to make it up to you."

"I love you, too, my little kitty," Jasper said as he lifted me up into his arms. I still clung to him for dear life, afraid he'd leave me for what I'd done. "We'll figure this out, Trey. I promise you, baby. I'm not mad at you. I just wish you didn't have to go through this. You deserve the two loving mates fate gave you."

"I don't need two, Jasper, I just want you," I replied as he moved us into the bedroom after toweling us both off. But as I said it, I felt my heart squeeze in my chest at the idea, and I realized it wasn't the truth. I think Jasper knew it, too, as he stared at me as he laid me down in bed. "I don't know if that's true."

"I know, Trey," he said as he moved into bed next to me and pulled the covers up around us. "But I'm glad you admitted that to me when you realized it. I'm grateful you won't lie to me no matter if what you're saying is painful."

"You are the one I love, Jasper," I whispered against his neck. "Addison might be my other mate, and I might need or want him. Maybe. But you are the one I love, my big wolf."

"I know that, my little kitty. I love you too," he said, kissing the top of my head as his hand rubbed my back. There really wasn't anything else to say. I lay there listening to his heart beat until I finally fell asleep.

Chapter 8

The next morning, Jasper and I made love. I cried the whole time as I told him how much I loved him, begging his forgiveness and not to leave me. Jasper swore he'd never leave me and we'd figure everything out together as mates should. When we climaxed together, I felt our souls intertwine. We held each other for a while afterwards while my mate was still inside me, connected to me.

After a bit we got out of bed and made breakfast together. I knew in my heart as I stared at the man who I loved more than life that he was telling the truth. Jasper would never leave me no matter how rough things got. Once we sat down, we talked about the situation as we ate. I told Jasper everything Addison had said to me and how he realized he'd messed up.

Jasper was quiet for a while, but finally said if I could find the ability to forgive Addison, he would too. He actually went so far as to suggest we try dating Addison. He might have realized his mistakes but Jasper wasn't sure that Addison was fully healed from his last relationship. He didn't want me to get hurt again or ruin what we had because we were trying to be mates with Addison.

I did believe Addison was sorry and felt guilty for how he'd handled our mating. But I also agreed with Jasper that Addison might not be ready for us. We decided to both think about what came next and not to do anything until we decided together. As we cleaned up the breakfast dishes, Jasper swore to me that no matter what happened he'd be there for me. Nothing would ever have him leaving me unless it was what I wanted.

Jasper's words warmed my heart as I headed to my office to get some work done. Honestly, after being in heat and the emotional toil the situation took on me, all I wanted to do was crawl back into bed with Jasper. But life goes on, and so did I.

I turned on my laptop as I rubbed my tired eyes, trying to shut off my personal life and focus on work. Starting with my Yahoo Group, I replied to messages and sent out updates. Then I worked on my Facebook posts, answering questions, and made sure to get my website current. It took a few hours to get all that done and check some of my latest reviews, but finally I got to my author account e-mails.

As it loaded up, I went to get another cup of coffee. The first e-mails were no big deal. A few contracts I needed to read and sign for new books, a cover design that I needed to approve, and finally some second-round edits for the two books I had coming out next month. In the middle of the e-mails there was one that I didn't want to open.

It was from a crazy fan who'd been emailing me for months. I'd never been able to track the guy down since it was just a random, generic e-mail that didn't tell me anything about the guy. At first he'd seemed normal, asking questions that just bordered on too personal.

Then the tone of the e-mails started changing when I wouldn't answer some of his questions. They started coming more often and were demanding. I stopped replying but saved them just in case it got out of hand. And I realized as I opened the e-mail and read it; we were finally at that point. I shook as I read the words over and over again.

"I know who you are now, Trey, and I'm going to show you the hot sex your stories need. Once I'm your master, you won't need to write books for everyone to see, only for my amusement."

He sent it to my author account but used my real name. How could he have found out who I was? I knew my publishers wouldn't have told anyone. They had a legal obligation with the contracts to keep their mouths shut. And I knew Jasper or my brothers would never tell. They were overly protective of me.

"Getting lots of work done, my little kitty?" Jasper asked as he joined me in the office. I didn't answer, not sure how to answer when I was so upset. "Trey? What's going on, baby?"

I opened my mouth several times to try and tell him, but I couldn't find the words. Instead, I looked at him over my shoulder and pointed to my laptop. In a flash, he was there with his arms wrapped around my shoulders as he read the e-mail.

"And this was sent to your pen name e-mail?" Jasper asked, and I nodded, still not having found my voice. I was up and out of the chair, in Jaspers arms before I could blink. Wrapping myself around him like a scared child, I tried to soak up some of his strength. "I have to ask, baby. Could this be Addison?"

"No, the e-mails started before I'd even met him," I answered finally as he carried me out of my office. "They didn't start like this, and this is the first one that uses my real name. I'm scared, Jasper."

"Don't be, my little kitty. I'd never let anything bad happen to you," he whispered as he sat me down on one of the kitchen table chairs. "I still want to call Addison and talk to him, okay?"

"Why?" I asked, looking up at him completely confused. "I don't think Addison even knows my pen name."

"Because you also got flowers from Addison," Jasper said gesturing to a large vase of flowers on the counter. "That's what I was coming to tell you. It might not be him, but they both came around the same time, okay? I want him to deny the e-mails are from him to my face so I can smell if he's lying."

"Okay," I whispered, pulling my knees to my chest on the chair. "His number's in my cell phone."

"We'll figure this out, Trey. No one's going to hurt you," Jasper said as he picked up my phone from the counter where we left our cells charging last night. I listened to what Jasper said, but I could feel the worry flowing off of him in waves. He clicked a few buttons on my phone and put it to his ear. My hearing as a shifter was strong enough that I could hear when Addison answered.

"Trey? Did you get my flowers?"

"He did, but this is Jasper."

"Oh, um, hi, Jasper," Addison said, sounding uncomfortable. "Is Trey okay?"

"No, he's not," Jasper replied, glancing over at me. "He's not injured or anything, but I need you to come to the house right now. We need to talk about something."

"Is this about last night?" Addison asked, cussing up a stream. "I knew we shouldn't have done that. It wasn't fair to Trey. I'm sorry, Jasper."

"This isn't about that, Addison," he assured our other mate, rubbing a hand over his face. "Look, can you just get over here as fast as possible. I need to talk to you and maybe show you something."

"I'm on duty, but nothing's going on, so, yeah, I'll be there in, like, five," Addison replied. They said their good-byes and hung up. Jasper made me some tea, watching me the whole time as if he was waiting for me to flip out. I tried to give him a smile, but I knew it was a weak attempt. When there was a knock at the door a little while later, he went to open it.

"Thanks for coming," Jasper said evenly as he let Addison in.

"Of course. I'm just a little confused as to why I'm here," he replied as he walked into the kitchen. Addison froze when he saw me and that gave me a glimpse as to how bad I must have looked then. He dropped to his knees in front of me and put his hands on my calves. "Trey, what's wrong, baby? Is this about last night? I'm so sorry, Trey. I shouldn't have let you do that for me. I fucked up again and I know flowers don't make up for that, but I wanted to send them anyway."

"It's not about last night, Addison," I said quietly as I put my tea on the table. I placed my hands over his on my legs as I watched him as I leaned my head on my knees. "What's my pen name, Addison?"

"Wait—what?" Addison asked, his eyebrows scrunching together as he looked taken aback. "What does that have to do with you being upset, Trey?"

"More than you know," Jasper answered for me. "Please answer the question, Addison. I think you can at least give Trey a little leeway after all that's happened."

"You're right, of course," Addison replied, nodding as he closed his eyes. It took him a few moments before he looked at me again. "I don't know. I'm not sure you ever told me. Any time we talked about your work, you always shut down on me."

"Because you were always telling me ways to do things better," I said softly, trying to keep this a calm conversation. "It was the same as criticizing me, like you knew how to be an author better than I did. It hurt and made me feel stupid."

"I–I didn't mean it like that, I swear," he replied, sitting back on his feet. Addison rubbed his hands over his face a few times before focusing on me again. "I'm sorry if that's how it came out, Trey. I wasn't trying to act like I knew more about being an author. I wanted to try and contribute to the conversations. Maybe help you if I could by giving you suggestions. God, I really screwed this all up. I should never have gone to Jeff for advice."

"What do you mean?" I asked, narrowing my eyes at him. "You told Jeff about our relationship?"

"I didn't tell him our personal business, no," Addison answered, shaking his head. "He'd always told me I never seemed interested in anything he did. So when we met, I didn't want to make the same mistakes with you. I asked Jeff how I could fix that and be better at showing you that I cared about your life than I had been with Jeff. He told me I should suggest ways to help make your life better."

Jasper let out a long whistle, getting both our attention as he leaned against the counter with his arms crossed over his chest.

"Look, I might not know much about relationships since this is my first with Trey," Jasper said, looking as if he was choosing his words carefully. "But that's advice I'd give someone if I was trying to tank their relationship, not make it stronger. I think this Jeff guy was trying to play you, Addison."

"Yeah, I kinda get that," Addison admitted to Jasper and then turned back to me. "None of this explains why you're upset or asked me here. So can you please tell me what's going on?"

"You think it was him?" I asked Jasper, waiting for him to shake his head. "I don't either."

"What was him? You mean me?" Addison asked, glancing between the two of us. "What wasn't me?"

"I've been getting some e-mails," I explained, taking a deep breath and looking at Jasper. "They've been coming from some whacked out fan before I even met either of you. When they started getting meaner and demanding, I ignored them. But I got one this morning that uses my real name, not my pen name. The guy says he knows who I am."

"And you wanted to make sure that I wasn't trying to fuck with you or create a situation where you'd need to call the police," Addison said, rubbing his chin. "Okay, I get that now."

"Actually, I never thought about that last one," I replied shaking my head. "You're too bad at hiding stuff or lying to have sent the e-mails in the hopes I'd call the police, Addison."

"Yeah, I've learned never to play poker," he snickered, giving me a wink. "I'd like to see these e-mails."

"The last one is up on my laptop, but I can pull the others too," I said as I stood up. I froze when I felt Addison stand and put his hand on my shoulder. Gazing up at him, I saw the conflicting emotions in his eyes.

"I know I fucked up and hurt you, Trey." Addison started to say, swallowing loudly before continuing. "But I really hope you know I could never intentionally hurt you or would mess with you like this. I didn't realize how what I was doing was wrong or affecting you. That's different than having the goal of upsetting you."

"I know that, Addy," I said softly and headed for the office. And I did. He fucked up because he was an idiot and let his past relationship leak into ours. That's not the same as beating me or trying to hurt me. They both followed me into the office as I sat down at my desk and pointed to the e-mail. I turned around when Addison gasped.

"Frank, it's Addison. Come back Frank," he said into the radio on his shoulder.

"What's up, dipshit?" Frank's voice came over the radio, and I had to bite my lip not to laugh.

"I need you over at Trey's new place right away."

"What did you do now, Addison?" Frank growled, his anger apparent. "So help me god, if you hurt that man again because your head's up your ass, I'm going to kick both!"

"This isn't a personal call, Frank," Addison answered, rolling his eyes. "I'm here in an official capacity. I'm calling in backup."

"Fuck! I'm flipping on the sirens. Be there in two," Frank said firmly. "Do I need to call Avery? What about EMS?"

"No, nothing like that, I just don't want to say it over the radio," Addison replied before releasing the button on the radio. He turned to me with concern in his eyes. "Can you print copies of all the e-mails out for us? Also, you might want to call Avery and his mates over here, Trey. The tone of this e-mail is threatening, and they know who you are. I think it's best if more than just Jasper and I know about this."

"I agree, baby," Jasper said quietly from behind us. "I think you'd feel better if your brother was here too."

"Will you call them?" I asked him, staring at the man I loved as the seriousness of the situation sank in. Jasper nodded and stepped out into the hallway to make the call as I opened all the e-mails and printed three copies. As they were printing, Addison rubbed my shoulders, and I leaned back to rest my head against his stomach. "I'm glad you're here, Addy."

"I wish this wasn't the reason you called me over, but I am too," he said softly, kissing the top of my head. "We'll fix this, okay? Jasper's a good man and protective of you. I know I was a jerk and bitched about you replacing me, but I really am glad you found him. You deserve to be happy and loved."

"I'm glad you think so, Addison," Jasper stated as he came back into the office. He glanced between the two of us, taking it in that we were touching. I realized he wasn't angry that I was touching Addison. He just looked leery. "Avery and his mates are on the way. I think Frank just pulled up."

"Let's start with these while the others print," Addison said as he grabbed the pages off the printer. I followed them into the living room as Jasper opened the door for Frank. After everyone greeted each other, Jasper moved towards me and wrapped his arms around me. I sighed and leaned back against his chest, soaking up his comfort while Addison filled Frank in.

"Trey?" I heard Avery call out as they got near the front door. Frank turned around to let them in and my brother raced through the open door to me. I hugged him fiercely as he tried to soothe me. "Jasper told us what's going on. Are you okay?"

"Mostly just in shock, I think," I answered as we parted. He eyed me over before giving me a quick nod and pulling me into the kitchen. I knew exactly what my little brother was going to say before he opened his mouth.

"And Addison is here why?" Avery asked, raising an eyebrow at me as he started to make some tea.

"Did you know that the full moon affects werewolves like it does us?" I asked him, seeing his eyes go wide as he put the pieces together. "Addison got drunk to try and take the edge off his need to reclaim me last night. And then showed up here banging on the door. Long story short, I let him reclaim me to stop his suffering."

"Fuck! Yeah, that's the best thing for you emotionally right now," Avery said shaking his head. "But why is he here now?"

"Because I wanted to make sure it wasn't Addison who's been sending the e-mails," Jasper answered as he joined us in the kitchen. "Can I get you anything, my little kitty? What can I do to help?"

"You're doing it, my big wolf," I said, rubbing my face against his chest as he hugged me. "After everyone leaves, I think I'm just going to try and get lost in work, if that's okay?"

"Whatever you need, baby," he whispered in my ear as he reached down and grabbed my ass. "Or if you want to be distracted, you know I'm always available for that."

"That has possibilities, too." I purred, smiling up at him.

"There's that smile I love." Jasper chuckled before giving me a deep kiss. "I'll do anything to see that smile on your face, baby."

"I know you will," I replied, kissing him back as everyone else joined us in the kitchen. I turned to face them as Jasper wrapped his arms around me and pulled me against his strong muscular chest. It made me feel so safe to be held by him. "So what do we do now?"

"We're going to bring your laptop in and call in some tech guys," Addison answered, glancing at Frank who nodded. "If you need to pull files off of it, I'd do that now. But we want to try and track down the guys IP address and see what we can find out."

"Okay, I can do that," I sighed, not liking the idea of getting even further behind on my work.

"We've got an extra laptop you can borrow," Cord said. I smiled at him. He was always so ready to help anyone out. He hid it well behind his tough exterior, but I'd seen him be incredibly gentle and loving with my brother.

"I'd appreciate that. The last thing I need is to get even further behind in work."

"Is there something Quinn could do to help?" Avery asked, and I wanted to kiss him then. Without even thinking about it, I pulled out of Jasper's arms and tackled my brother. We fell back against the floor and I peppered his face with kisses as we wrestled.

"You're a friggin' genius, Avery!" I squealed as we both sat back up. We started giggling like goofs when we saw all the others staring at us like we'd lost it. I decided to take pity on them and explain. "Our brother Quinn is an author in the same genre as me."

"There we go." Jasper snickered as he rolled his eyes. "I was waiting for the rest of that thought and why you got so excited."

"He can't write my books for me," I said with a shrug. "But he knows my style, and we've helped each other out with edits and what not when we've had deadlines. I was too distracted by the hotness of my big wolf when we met and then in heat to even think of asking him for help."

"The hotness of your big wolf, huh?"

"He's very hot and I love the feeling of his cock in me." I answered in our mating link. I stood up and reached down to help Avery as Jasper replied.

"I've still not felt that tiger tongue licking my ass, my little kitty. I think it might be time to do some playing after everyone leaves. I have need for my mate."

I instantly got hard and moved to my mate, purring loudly as I rubbed against his massive body. *"Maybe I should make you my tiger tongue slut?"*

"Behave, my little kitty," Jasper groaned as he slapped my ass, getting another purr from me. I heard what sounded like some sniffling and turned to look over my shoulder. Addison was staring at us, tears spilling out of his eyes before he turned and left. I felt my heart breaking as the front door closed behind him.

"Shit." I hissed, feeling my own tears forming. "I wasn't thinking. I didn't mean to be an ass in front him like that."

"Addison did this to himself, Trey," Frank said firmly. "He needs to deal with the consequences of it. Besides, you were the one who got hurt and have the drama going on. You shouldn't have to tiptoe around his feelings."

"Yeah, but I didn't have to flaunt using our mental link in front of him either." I sighed as Jasper's arms enclosed around me. I buried my face into his chest feeling his pain at the situation as much as mine. We had to figure this out once we got past this thing with the e-mails. All three of us were hurting. And who did that really help?

Chapter 9

I was working on my latest story with Cord's borrowed laptop that night. Jasper was resting next to me on our bed. He'd asked my why I'd decided to write there, and I'd answered him that right now my office held bad feelings for me. Jasper smiled softly at me and promised that after this was over we'd have another fantasy time and put the good feelings back in there. I knew he meant it too. That's just how Jasper was.

The next e-mail came then, and I felt myself go cold. Reaching over, I gave Jasper's shoulder a shake before I opened it. He opened his eyes and smiled at me until he saw that I was pointing to the computer. Jasper sat up, put his arm around me and nodded that he was ready.

"Call your cop mate again, and I'll kill both of your mates and take you for my slave. You will learn to obey me, Trey."

I started shaking uncontrollably. Pushing the laptop off me, I leapt off the bed, and raced to the bathroom. I barely made it in time before I threw up the contents of my stomach. Jasper held me as I kept vomiting until there was nothing left and I was just dry heaving. I slumped back against him then, and he wiped my mouth with a wet towel.

"You need to leave, Jasper," I whispered staring up at him. His eyes got wide, and I realized he thought something other than what I meant. "I won't risk you. I can't risk you because some freak is after me."

"Baby, wild horses couldn't drag me out of here when you need me most," Jasper said firmly taking my face in his hands. "I'm not scared of this fuck nut. He will not take me away from you or you from me, okay?"

"Okay," I said quietly knowing he wouldn't leave. I rubbed my face over his perfect chest, purring as I tried to comfort him as he was me. "We need to call Addison."

"Yeah, I'll handle it," Jasper replied as he stood with me in his arms. "You're going to get some rest, my little kitty. Let me take care of you, please, Trey?"

"Only if you join me after you're done," I said begging him with my eyes that he understood that I needed his big protective arms around me.

"Absolutely. I need to hold my baby right now," he replied giving me a quick kiss. It might have been true, but he said the words out loud because I needed to hear it.

Jasper pulled his phone out of his pocket, and I listened as he filled Addison in. They decided that Addison should not come over right then and risk pissing this guy off anymore. Instead, Jasper took the laptop and forwarded the message to him.

After they hung up, Jasper put away the laptop and crawled into bed with me. I went to him instantly, laying against him. That wasn't enough for him. Jasper pulled me on top of him and moved my legs between his. His strong arms held me as I laid my head on his shoulder.

"I love you, Jasper," I whispered as I kissed his neck.

"I love you, too, my little kitty," he replied as he nuzzled my head. "I won't ever leave you, Trey. And I won't let anyone take you from me."

* * * *

The next day I was alone and locked up in the house. Jasper hadn't wanted leave me, but he had to help Ty and Cord for a little bit and order supplies for their horses now that the sale had gone through. We'd talked about the offer my brother's mates had made.

I could see the excitement in Jasper's eyes as he told me about the horses, and I knew this was what my mate was born to do with his life. He admitted there was a lot more horses than he was used to working with but that the offer compensated him handsomely for the time he'd be putting in.

My only stipulation was that they work with him when I was in heat, and Jasper assured me that they'd already talked about that. He'd work six days a week but always have the lunar cycle off to make sure his mate was taken care of. I had smiled at him and handed him the phone. He called them and put it on speaker so I could hear everything as he'd accepted the offer.

Jasper was gone about an hour when I realized I really needed to get some contracts in the mail. My publishers would start getting upset for me that I'd been sitting on them for the past couple of weeks. I printed them out quickly, read them over, signed them, and got them into an envelope. As I headed out the front door, I made sure to look around as I sniffed the air to make sure I was really alone.

I drove over to the post office, on high alert the entire time. I pulled into the parking lot and got out of the car, sniffing the air. Smelling multiple scents, I realized I might be overreacting. It was the middle of the day. Who would be bold enough to try anything in the middle of town?

Unfortunately I got my answer as I walked around the building from the back parking lot to the entrance. Someone grabbed me from behind and covered my mouth before I could scream.

"Try to shift, and I will tear out your throat before you can," the man growled in my ear. And it hit me like a ton of bricks. I knew that voice and his scent. It was the Beta from the local pack, Gregg. "You're mine now, Trey."

I struggled against his hold in sheer panic as he dragged me over to an alley where no one could see us. He pushed up against a building hard as he inserted himself in between my legs. Removing his hand from my mouth, I went to scream, but he pressed his mouth to mine. Not knowing what else to do, I bit him.

"Fucking little slut," he growled out, smacking me hard across the face. A human I could have pushed away and fought off, but he was another shifter and I was in human form.

"No, please don't do this," I cried out as he groped my groin hard. His hand slapped back over my mouth, the force of it causing the back of my head to hit the brick wall. I screamed and fought as he tore my pants and tried to touch me. Before he could, as quickly as Gregg appeared, he was suddenly pulled off of me. I slid down against the wall and pulled my knees to my chest.

"That's my mate," I heard Addison growl as I curled into a ball. I peeked up to see that they had both shifted into half man, half wolf forms and started fighting. Part of me was frozen in fear while the rest of me was screaming to call for help. Not sure I could use my voice right then, I pulled out my phone and typed out a quick text. I sent it to Jasper, Avery, Cord, Ty, and Frank, praying someone was close enough to help.

The sick sound of bones breaking got me coherent enough to finally focus on the fight in front of me. Addy was standing on shaky legs as he shifted back, his uniform in tears. Gregg lay in a pile against the other building, twisted in such a way that no living person could.

"It's over, baby," Addison said gently as he took the last few steps towards me. "You're safe. Gregg's dead. He won't ever hurt you."

"Addy!" I cried out as I leapt into his arms. He caught me as I wrapped my entire body around him, sobbing.

"Shh, I'm here, baby." Addison said over and over again as he comforted me. He rubbed his hands over my back as he kissed my temple every so often. As I started to calm down, I remembered he'd been the one fighting.

"Oh, my god, I'm sorry." I gasped, pulling away from him as I started to search his body. "Are you okay, Addy? Did he hurt you?"

"I'm fine, baby. As long as you're safe, I'm perfectly fine," he answered as he rubbed my cheek. I started purring uncontrollably as my mate, who'd just saved me, comforted me. Before he could say anything else, the cavalry arrived. Jasper was the first one to reach us, racing down the alley.

"Are you okay, Trey?" he asked as he skidded to a stop. Addison lowered me to my feet without being asked and stepped away enough so Jasper could see every inch of me. He must have seen my torn pants because tears formed in his eyes. "Did he?"

"No, Jasper, he didn't rape me. Addison showed up in time to save me," I whispered as I hugged my mate. Right then he needed more comforting than I did. The fear was pouring off of him in waves. "I'm okay, Jasper. I'm fine, I swear. Addison got here in time."

"Thank god," Jasper cried, squeezing me tighter. He turned so we could both see Addison who looked lost. "How did you get here in time? Did you figure out it was Gregg?"

"Um, no," Addison said, blushing furiously as he started at his feet. Jasper went stiff and let go of me as he faced Addison. After a moment, he looked back up at us. "I've been watching the house from a distance since the e-mail yesterday. When Trey left, I followed him. I would have gotten here sooner, but I didn't want him to see me and get pissed so I parked in another parking lot. I'm sorry I didn't stop it sooner."

Jasper went to Addison then, and I was scared he was going to be pissed that he'd followed me. Instead, my big wolf shocked me down to my toes. He reached for Addison and kissed him fiercely. Addison gasped, but kissed Jasper back. They pulled apart for a moment, staring at each other. This time, Addison pulled Jasper to him. I got hard watching my two mates making out as they were all hands and lips.

"Thank you, Addy," Jasper panted against Addison's lips after they parted. "Thank you for putting our mate before yourself and protecting him."

"I'd do anything to keep him safe," Addy told Jasper, but glanced at me. "I didn't know how you'd react to my watching you after everything that happened. But I wasn't with you like Jasper was, and you're still my mate, Trey. It was killing me that I wouldn't be able to keep you safe if need be."

I stared at him for several moments as his words sunk in as well as what Jasper had said. After watching them make out like that, I knew what the next thing to do was, and I blurted it out.

"Will you go out with us, Addy?" I asked, glancing at Jasper who smiled widely. Addison's eyes went wide as he let go of Jasper and moved towards me. Then he smiled so big that it reached his eyes.

"Can I get a kiss before this date?"

"After what you did to protect me," I purred as I took a step forward and rubbed my body against his. "Abso-fucking-lutely."

Addy wrapped his arms around me as he gently touched his lips to mine. It wasn't enough for me. I dragged his head back down as I threw my arms around his neck and licked his lips. He groaned and opened for me. I kept purring as our tongues rubbed against each other's and intertwined.

"Fuck, am I turned on right now," Jasper grumbled as Frank, Avery, and his mates showed up. I parted with Addy in time to catch my brother as he ran towards me.

"Never again, Trey," Avery cried in between hiccups. "You can't ever scare me like that again, brother."

"I promise," I said gently as I held him tight. I knew I'd been the one almost raped and kidnapped, but after everything Avery had been through, he couldn't take any more pain and drama in his life. And I knew in his heart that part of Avery would die if any of his brothers had to suffer what he'd been through.

"It was Gregg?" Frank asked, looking past us at the crumpled body. "Well, that's just fucking great. One of our own goddamn pack. I'll call Alpha Daniels and the Sheriff. You guys make yourselves scarce before we draw a crowd."

Jasper swung me up into his arms, but paused as he stared at Addy. I reached out my hand and our other mate smiled widely at us as he took it. Jasper carried me back to the parking lot with Addy at our side. And for the first time, I truly felt at peace with both of my mates next to me. Just the way it should be.

Chapter 10

We'd gone out the next night on our first date with Addy. It had been perfect. When we'd gotten home, Jasper and I agreed that neither of us liked the idea of our other mate not being there with us. But still, we took it slower this time around. And it was working out great.

Addy and Jasper ended up getting along, and after the third date, we invited Addy to spend the night with us. I'd gotten so horny watching them make out I ended up shifting into my half and half form and eating out both their asses. Then I stroked myself as I watched Jasper fuck Addy into the mattress.

By the fifth date, Addy and Jasper had claimed each other, and Addy started spending nights at our house. After two weeks, we all sat down to have a long talk about the future. We'd all agreed that the right move was for Addy to move in with us if he wanted this to work.

There were too many bad memories in his house for us to work out, plus the house we were renting was bigger. Addy would move in most of his furniture since we were still lacking, but with one stipulation—we'd keep our bed that Jasper and I met on.

It was the first day of the next lunar cycle Addy moved in. We'd gotten most of the boxes in already, but I excused myself when I felt that I was going into heat. I quickly showered and got myself stretched out as they carried in the furniture. When I was done, I snuck into the spare bedroom and pulled out my phone. Deciding to have some fun with both of them, I sent them the same text message.

I'm naked, stretched out, in heat, and waiting in the office to play the next game with my mates.

Seconds later they were tripping over each other as they raced into the room. They stared at me for a moment as I started purring and stroking my cock. Then they glanced at each other before pulling off their clothes.

"I need some help with a threesome sex scene in my book," I said softly as I dropped to my knees. I batted my eyelashes up at them as I spread my legs wide and tilted my head submissively. "I was hoping my mates would help me do some research."

"What kind of research, baby?" Addy asked as he unzipped his pants and his hard cock slapped up against his stomach.

"I need to know if I can be a cock slut to two men," I said, purring loudly as I licked my lips. "I'm in heat and begging for cock. Will my mates please, please, *please* help me and let me suck on their gorgeous cocks?"

"Yeah, like I'm going to say no to an offer like that." Addy snickered as he kicked off his shoes, pulled down his jeans and boxer briefs. All Jasper had left was his shirt that he whipped off.

"Are you ready to purr, beg, and scream for us if we agree to let you be our cock slut, baby?" Jasper asked, his voice demanding. I saw Addy look at him like he'd lost it before glancing back at me. Jasper gave him a sideways look after I'd nodded my acceptance. "We played this game last lunar cycle. Trey role plays the sub, begging to be spanked and to be our cock slut. And I get to live out my fantasy of being his research material for his hot sex scenes."

"I like this fantasy." Addy growled, watching me intently as I crawled over to him. When I was at his feet, I sat back on my heels as I ran my hands up his thighs, getting a shiver from him.

"Please, Addy. I need cock," I begged, purring loudly. "Make me your cock slut before you both fuck me on my desk. Your mate has been very bad and needs to be spanked, then fucked hard."

"Oh, fuck, I love this game." Addy moaned as he grabbed his cock. I opened my mouth as I kept purring, my eyes never leaving his. He ran the big mushroom head around my lips before pushing it into my mouth. I purred as I ran my tongue around it before swallowing it down as much as I could. "I'm not sure my knees will hold me up for this."

"I have the answer for that." Jasper chuckled as he walked past us. I heard my desk move as I sucked on my mate's cock. Strong arms wrapped around me, and I squeaked as I was lifted up. I purred when I saw that he'd moved it to the middle of the room. He laid me face down on the desk. "Let us know if we go too far, okay, my little kitty?"

"I promise," I answered with a wink before getting back into character. "Please, I need cock. Punish your mate and fuck my mouth and ass."

"Like this?" Jasper growled as his hand landed on my ass hard. I moaned and spread my legs wider for him. Addy came around the other side of the desk, holding his dick out to me.

"Suck me off like the little cock slut you are, baby," he ordered so sternly that I shivered. I winked up at him as I swallowed him back down. I rotated between moaning and purring as Addy thrust himself into my mouth as Jasper kept spanking me. "Oh, our little mate likes this game."

"We decided it was something different to start off the fun when he goes into heat," Jasper said before his hand landed hard on my ass and sac. I moaned wildly, taking Addy all the way down my throat. His trimmed pubic hairs tickled my nose, but I was too focused on the taste of him to care. "I think our little kitty likes his sac spanked, as well. Is that right, baby?"

I groaned as I tried to nod as I licked and sucked on the cock in my mouth. Jasper was more than willing to give me what I wanted, though he was careful not to smack my balls as hard as he did my ass.

"Would you like to spank our mate, Addy?" Jasper asked, seeing that Addy was close to coming. "I could use a good blow job right now."

"I could get behind the idea of spanking our naughty little cock slut," Addy snickered at his own pun. I groaned as he pulled out of my mouth and traded places. "Did you notice our baby stretched and lubed himself up for us, Jasper?"

"I did, and I think he should be rewarded for that, don't you?" Jasper said, staring down at me as I looked up at him and purred.

"I agree," Addy said as he rubbed his hands over my ass, getting a gasp from me as heat radiated out and to my dick.

"What do you want for your reward, Trey?"

I knew what I wanted, but I didn't know how to ask for it. So instead, I felt my face heat up, probably as red as my ass, as I looked away from him.

"Hey, now," Jasper said gently as he knelt down in front of me so his face was right in front of mine. He cupped my cheek gently and turned me back to him, his eyes filled with concern. "Are you not enjoying this, Trey? We can stop if you aren't?"

"No, I am it's j–just," I stuttered out and took a deep breath. "You asked me what I wanted as my reward, and I don't know how to tell you."

"You can tell us anything, Trey," Addy said gently as he moved around me to kneel next to Jasper. "We've told you our fantasies, and you're giving it to both of us. If there's something you want, we want to give it to you as well."

"Okay," I whispered as I looked at both the men I loved. It hit me then how I could get Jasper to figure it out without having to say it out loud. "Do you remember the last time we played this and I suggested something for the next time?"

"That's what you want?" Jasper asked, getting a feral grin on his lips. I blushed even harder as I nodded, glancing at Addy.

"But I want both of us to suck your cock while Addy's in me," I whispered, closing my eyes in embarrassment.

"That's so fucking hot." Jasper moaned before kissing me. I gasped in surprise, opening my eyes and kissing him back. He stood and helped me up off the desk as he looked at Addy. "Trey suggested that he get spanked while I sat on his desk chair as he rode me. It seems he adjusted his fantasy to include you."

"And I'm ever so grateful for that," Addy whispered, his eyes filling up with tears. In a flash we were both hugging our mate, rubbing his back. Addy looked at me first, and then Jasper before declaring how he felt for us. "I love you, Trey. I love you, too, Jasper. You both are the best mates anyone could ever have asked for."

"Did you tell him?" I asked Jasper, who smiled and shook his head. I looked back at Addy's confused face, and I explained. "Jasper told me he loved me last lunar cycle before we started playing. He said I was his perfect fantasy, and he loved me for being willing to give him what he wanted."

"And now you're doing the same," Jasper said quietly. "And we love you, too, Addy."

"Really?" He gasped, hugging us both. "Thank you for giving me another chance."

"It's what you do for your mate," I replied nodding. "And someone you love."

"Now where were we?" Jasper asked after a few more moments of our group hug. "Oh, I know. Our little cock slut is going to ride Addy's cock."

"Please, I need it so bad," I begged, rubbing against Addy suggestively. He grabbed my arm and dragged me onto his lap as he sat down on my chair. I purred loudly as he moved his hands to my hips and lifted me up so that his hard cock brushed against my hole. "Give me your cock, Addy. I want it hard while we suck on Jasper's cock. I need so much cock when I'm in heat."

"Gladly," Addy growled, pulling my hips down hard as he thrust up into me. We both groaned as he bottomed out inside of me.

Jasper didn't miss a beat as he stepped up next to us. The height of the chair wasn't right, so Addy pulled the lever on the side of it and the chair went lower. With Jasper being as tall as he was, it worked out then. I greedily purred and licked Jasper's cock as I moved my hips.

"No one said you could move yet, baby," Addy said sternly as he smacked my ass. I moaned wildly and tried to take all of Jasper into my mouth. That got me another slap. "You're not begging for it."

"Please, please. I need my mate's big cocks," I whimpered, licking Jasper's cock every time I took Addy all the way into me. I purred loudly when Jasper pushed his dick into my mouth, Addy spanked me as I kept riding him. It was perfect, and kinky, and everything I'd ever fantasized about.

"Oh, yeah. Suck me harder, my little kitty," Jasper groaned, thrusting his hips forward. He moved his hand to the back of my head so he could control how deeply I took him, and I gladly gave it over to him. "That's it. Take all of me, Trey."

"We should think about getting toys or a paddle for our baby," Addy grunted out in between helping lick Jasper's dick. I pulled back off of him, and Jasper slid his cock in between our mouths as we both sucked and licked it. Groaning when I felt Addy's tongue slide over mine as we licked Jasper, he grabbed my left hip to help me. He used his left hand to spank me, and I felt myself getting close with all the sensations to my body.

"I need to come," I panted, holding onto Addy's shoulders for better leverage. "Please, please, let me come."

"I think he's been good enough, don't you Addy?" Jasper asked as he started to stroke my cock as I rode Addy harder and harder.

"Oh, yeah. Come for us baby. We want to hear you scream in pleasure," Addy demanded, spanking me hard. That's all it took to throw me over the edge. I threw back my head and screamed loudly, giving my mates what they wanted as I shot my load all over Jasper's hand and Addy's stomach. Addy followed me right over, thrusting up into me hard as he cried out my name.

"We're not done with you yet, my little kitty." Jasper growled as my orgasm started to ebb. He moved behind me and spanked me hard several times in a row as Addy was still coming. I leaned forward to give him better access to my ass as I purred loudly. The second Addy nodded at Jasper that his climax was done, Jasper pulled me off of Addy as I groaned. "Do you want more cock in this sweet ass, baby?"

"Yes," I hissed, feeling my cock taking notice again already after I'd just finished. Jasper laid me on the desk with my ass hanging off. He lifted my legs up so my ankles rested on his shoulders as he thrust into my ass hard. I cried out, loving the feeling of him needing me so desperately. "Give me that big cock, Jasper. Fuck your mate as hard as you can."

"Dirty, dirty little cock slut, Jasper chuckled, winking down at me as he started pounding into my ass. Reaching over my head, I grabbed onto the side of the desk to hold myself in place as I started to slide across it. "You feel like heaven, my little kitty."

"Harder, Jasper. I need more," I begged, wanting him to spank me more. He smiled, knowing exactly what I wanted, and I gasped as his hand landed on my ass. I moaned loudly as my head thrashed from side to side on the desk. It spurred my mate on. Jasper growled like the wolf he was and fucked me even harder. I saw Addy get up off the chair as he moved around to my head.

"Watching you two is just too hot not to get hard again," he said with a shrug as he fed me his cock. I groaned at the taste of him. Addy pinched my nipples, and suddenly I was on sensation overload.

With one cock in my mouth, one in my ass, and one mate spanking me while the other pinched my nipples, my orgasm hit me out of nowhere like a freight train. I screamed around the dick in my mouth as both mates watched me.

"So fucking beautiful, baby." Jasper grunted and then roared out his release as he pounded into me. Addy was seconds behind us and I greedily swallowed every drop of his cum. He braced a hand on the desk, as did Jasper, so no one crushed me. Addy pulled his now spent dick out of my mouth as Jasper did the same from my ass. All that could be heard for several moments was all three of us panting.

"That was even better than I'd pictured in my head," I said, smiling up at them when I'd caught my breath. "We so have to play this game again."

"You won't have to twist my arm." Jasper chuckled as he lifted me into his arms. Addy nodded as he leaned over to kiss me. Jasper walked us out of my office and into our bathroom with Addy following. He set me on my feet in the shower and turned on the water. I reached for the soap, but Addy beat me to it.

"This is still your fantasy, Trey. Let us wash you and take care of you," Jasper said as way of an explanation.

"Every day with my mates is my perfect fantasy," I replied, kissing him and then Addy. "And you always take care of me."

"It's what you do for someone you love," Addy said, using my earlier words as he moved to hug me from behind.

"And we do love you, my little kitty," Jasper added as he hugged me from the front. And there, sandwiched between my two loving mates I finally felt that everything had worked out. This was how being mated was supposed to be. And didn't that just make me the luckiest kitty ever?

THE END

WWW.JOYEEFLYNN.COM

ABOUT THE AUTHOR

Joyee Flynn grew up in Chicago living in the same house all her life until she left for college. She loves to get lost in fantasy that only books could bring. She kept writing, short stories, romance, mystical, and of course adding in hot cowboys any chance she could. Her wide interest in reading was reflected in her writings. Currently Joyee lives with her dog, Marius, named after a vampire from Ann Rice's *Interview with the Vampire* series. She dreams of one day living out in Montana, enough land to have a few horses, and find a couple of cowboys of her own.

A lover of men, Joyee's all about them in any form in her books. Vampire, werewolf, military, doesn't matter at all as long as they are hot, hard, and sex fiends!

Also by Joyee Flynn

Also by Stormy Glenn and Joyee Flynn

Available at
BOOKSTRAND.COM

Siren Publishing, Inc.
www.SirenPublishing.com

Breinigsville, PA USA
14 April 2011
259868BV00004B/194/P